On my father's retu_____ a
flimsy dressing-gown _____ _____ _____ Lucette,
who was in equally casual attire. They were careful to
close the door and draw the curtain, but my preparations frustrated their precautions, at least in part. As
soon as they were in the room, I was at the door with
my face glued to the glass by the lifted curtain. The
first person to meet my eyes was Lucette with her
magnificent bosom completely bare. It was so
seductive that I could not blame my father for
immediately covering it with quick, eager kisses.
Unable to hold himself back, he tore off her clothing,
and in a twinkling of an eye, skirt, blouse and chemise
were on the floor. How temptingly lovely she was in
her natural state! I could not tear my eyes from her . . .

THE LIFTED CURTAIN
&
MY CONVERSION

Le Comte de Mirabeau

Translation by Howard Nelson
Introduction by J–P Spencer

A Nexus Book
First published in 1986
This edition published 1990
by the Paperback Division of
W H Allen & Co plc
Unit 26, Grand Union Centre,
338 Ladbroke Grove, London W10 5AH

Translation Copyright © Holloway House Publishing Co 1972
Introduction copyright © J–P Spencer 1986

Printed and bound in Great Britain by
Cox & Wyman Ltd, Reading

ISBN 0 352 32494 5

INTRODUCTION

Within these pages you will encounter a voice that speaks across two centuries, from behind the prison walls of the Château de Vincennes in the dying days of the *ancien régime* in France. It belongs to a young nobleman of singular talent and personality who is destined to play a significant role in the complex political turmoil that lies just a few years off and which is known as the French Revolution. But, as yet, Comte Gabriel Honoré Riqueti de Mirabeau rots in prison at the instigation of his father, separated from the woman he loves and their child – whom he will never see – and seeks an outlet for his prodigious energies.

Born on 9th March 1749, despite his position as the eldest son of a noble family, Mirabeau cannot be said to have enjoyed a privileged childhood. By virtue of his boisterous character and his striking ugliness – worsened by the scars of small-pox contracted at the age of three – Mirabeau was at constant loggerheads with his father, the Marquis de Mirabeau. As befitted a leading economic and social philosopher of his time, the Marquis' own finances were in permanent disorder and his family lived in complete disharmony. Mirabeau's mother left home when he was thirteen and she was replaced by his father's mistress who was unsuccessful in her attempts to act as stepmother to a boy already written off by his father as 'likely to be nothing but an incurably perverse idiot'.

The conflict between father and son raged throughout Mirabeau's adolescence and early manhood but, however harsh the punishment enforced by the Marquis, it was never enough to halt Gabriel's excesses. His entry into the cavalry at the age of eighteen ended in a welter of debts, an anguished love affair and imprisonment under a *lettre de cachet* enforced by his father. These *lettres* simply sidestepped the usual channels of justice and thrust the unfortunate recipient behind the walls of a state prison such as the Bastille or, in Mirabeau's case, the Isle de Ré in 1768, Château d'If in 1774, Fort de Joux in 1775 and the Château de Vincennes in 1777. Each of these periods of imprisonment was brought about by the Marquis, though sometimes the *lettres* were enforced to enable Mirabeau to escape worse punishment – for when a man was in the hands of the king's own special brand of justice he was also, fortunately, beyond the reach of his creditors.

It was during his term in the Fort de Joux, near Pontarlier, in the Jura, that Mirabeau met the grand passion of his life – Sophie de Monnier, the young wife of a local nobleman some forty-eight years her senior. Ironically it was Saint-Mauris, Mirabeau's jailer, who introduced the lovers, for the ageing Saint-

Mauris himself had designs on the bored and nubile young lady. Sophie later said that when she first met Mirabeau she did not know if he was ugly or handsome – in any event they both fell heavily in love and a tortuous intrigue began which culminated in their elopement on the night of 24th August 1776. They set up home in Amsterdam, where Mirabeau set to work in the publishing trade and Sophie gave Italian lessons. Meanwhile, in France, the abandoned relatives of both parties set about bringing the lovers to heel. In May 1777 they were arrested and brought back to France; Mirabeau was despatched to the Château de Vincennes and the pregnant Sophie was taken to a house of correction.

Unlike the Fort de Joux, Vincennes was a real prison and Mirabeau was confined in a room ten feet by ten, forbidden even to converse with the turnkey who brought his food. He did, however, have access to books and during the ensuing years (he was released in December 1780) he gradually won concessions in the conditions of his imprisonment. Chief among these was the right to correspond with Sophie and, in these letters, references can be found to the erotic work which formed a part of his considerable literary output of the time.

In his letter of 2nd February 1780 Mirabeau tells Sophie of his idea of writing a novel based on the theme of a cynical young stud who has renounced beauty and now proposes to fuck only for money. 'The notion is crazy but the details are delightful and I'll read it to you some day at the risk of having my eyes scratched out.' On the 5th March he says that if he were a bookseller the novel would make his fortune.

He offers Sophie a copy to read and asserts that it is less frivolous than it might appear at first glance, though 'I can't reread it without laughing.' On the 26th March comes the final reference to the book which he maintains is a true picture of the morals of the time. He also says, 'In prison you must make desperate efforts to be merry and to force yourself to exist. Otherwise you will soon be discouraged, and dead or mad.'

The novel referred to in these letters was first published in 1783 under the title *Ma Conversion* and its author was identified by the initials M.D.R.C.D.M.F. (Monsieur de Riqueti, Comte de Mirabeau fils). The second edition appeared the following year as *The Libertine of Quality* or *Secrets of a Prisoner in the Château of Vincennes*; it bore no author's name. The third edition in 1790, simply called *The Libertine of Quality*, was the first to credit Mirabeau. It was followed in 1791, after Mirabeau's death, by an edition designed to cash in on his celebrity, and, if Apollinaire and others are to be believed, to besmirch his reputation, since it carries a lengthy list of titles beneath his name – '*deputé du Tiers-État des Sénéchaussées d'Aix et de Marseille, membre du département de Paris, commandant de bataillon de la milice bourgeoise du district de Grang-Batellière, président du club jacobite, etc., etc.*' Many other French editions, mostly on a small scale, have followed since – some of which have been the subject of legal censure.

Despite its robust and ribald tone and the cheerfully obscene behaviour of its protagonists, *My Conversion* is less of an erotic novel than an act of literary revenge. Up to the point of writing – and as remained the case

8

until his election in 1789 as the deputy for Aix – Mirabeau's life had been spent in a quest for meaningful work. He had many talents – literary facility, forceful intellect and personal dynamism – yet he was forever on the outside looking in. *My Conversion* paints a scabrous portrait of the insiders – ladies of the court, the nobility, tradeswomen, nuns, monks – and doubtless the writing of it relieved frustrations born of his long years of rejection and imprisonment.

The companion to *My Conversion* in this volume, *The Lifted Curtain* or *Laura's Education*, has a much less certain history. Some experts dispute Mirabeau's authorship though the French authority Louis Perceau ascribes the work to the prisoner of Vincennes and it is included in the omnibus edition of Mirabeau's *Erotic Works* published by Fayard and L'Enfer de la Bibliothèque Nationale (the equivalent of the Private Case of the British Library) in 1984. Though intrinsically less interesting than *My Conversion*, considered purely as a piece of erotic writing it is more effective. The notion of a young girl embarking on her sexual education at the hands of her father (who, in fact, is *not* her father) plays on the taboo of incest – a theme particularly popular with English writers of erotica in the Victorian era.

By the time Mirabeau regained his liberty it seems his love for Sophie had faded. He resumed his life as a philandering adventurer, living off his wits and his pen, always in debt, always in search of a lucrative commission. He travelled to England with his new mistress Henriette de Nehra in 1784; in 1786 he was in Berlin authorized by Talleyrand to spy on the Prussian court. It was not, however, until 1789 and the election for the Estates-General, that Mirabeau found his true calling. He was a brilliant public speaker, destined to become the finest orator of the Revolution, and he won the support of the voters of Aix-en-Provence in April 1789.

The history of the French Revolution is confusing and complex but from the time of his election until his death almost exactly two years later, Mirabeau erased the poor opinion of his character that his libertine life had thus far earned him, won a place in the history books and died a hero of the people. At heart a democratic monarchist, he tried to build a bridge between the old order and a new constitution in which the king would play a part. It is even possible that his cunning politicking would have succeeded and thus altered the course of history if his much abused constitution had not finally collapsed on 2nd April. His funeral procession was three miles long and it contained his political enemies as well as his many friends. It was not until midnight on 4th April 1791 that it finally reached its destination, the recently completed church of Sainte-Genevieve – the Pantheon – which was now to be the resting place of the nation's heros. Mirabeau was the first man to be honoured in this way – final redemption for the Libertine of Quality.

J–P Spencer

The Lifted Curtain, or Laura's Education

Part One

I was fifteen years old when my mother was seized with an illness which proved to be fatal. After eight months of suffering, she left this life. Realizing the depth of my sorrow at the loss, my father cherished me all the more, and I returned his tenderness with all my heart.

I was continually the object of his caresses. Not a day passed without his cuddling me and covering my face and lips with the most passionate kisses.

I remember that my mother had reproached him one day for the liberties he was taking with my body.

'What are you complaining about, Madame?' he had replied. 'I am doing nothing wrong. If she were my daughter, the censure would be justified. I am no Lot.'

This incident never left my memory, although I did not understand until some time later. I clung to him, however, since I knew I owed everything to him. It was not hard to do, for he was the soul of affection and solicitude.

So favoured was I by nature that he believed that the deity of love had fashioned me. He never tired of telling that to me. From my infancy, I showed promise of a pleasing, svelte figure and a face with regular features. The vivacity of my brown eyes was tempered by the sweetness of my glance. Although I was lively and gay, I had a tendency to be reflective.

My father studied carefully my tastes and inclinations, which he cultivated and developed with the greatest diligence. One thing that he was insistent on was that I hold nothing back from him. It was a condition I found no difficulty in meeting. His tenderness for me was such that on the infrequent occasions when he thought I deserved to be punished, the blows were caresses.

Some time after the death of my mother, he took me in his arms.

'Laurette, my dear child,' he said, 'It is now time to think of your education.'

With my father as my sole teacher, I received the most brilliant training imaginable. He was familiar with everything – drawing, dancing, music, literature and the sciences.

Although my father was occupied with my upbringing, I noticed him often sunk deep in thought and perturbed. It was obvious that something was bothering him. After my mother's demise, we had left our home in the country to live in the city. Since he had few other interests, I became the centre of his life and the object of all his affection.

The caresses he lavished on me seemed to animate him, for his eyes sparkled, his face turned red, and his lips became dry and hot. He liked to take my buttocks in his hands and massage them. Or he passed a finger over my thighs while he kissed my mouth and breast. Often, he completely undressed me and lowered my naked body into a bath. After having dried me and rubbed oils and essences into my skin, he put his lips to every part of my body excepting one. As he contemplated me, he shook all over. Then his hands were again on me. How I liked this delightful game. Then suddenly he ceased his fiery manipulations to run and lock himself in his study.

One day, when his kisses were more impassioned than usual, kisses I returned with my usual tenderness, and our mouths were glued together with his tongue moistening my lips, I suddenly felt strange sensations. The flame of his embraces had slipped into my veins. He then escaped me when I least expected it and great was my chagrin. Also, I was curious to learn what had attracted him to his room, but when I tried to open the door, I found it latched.

The following day, he was given a letter which seemed to please him. After having read it a second time, he spoke to me.

'My dear Laura, it is time for you to have a governess. One is arriving tomorrow. Although she comes with the highest recommendations, I have to see her for myself to make my own judgment if they are exaggerated or not.'

I was totally unprepared for such news which, for some reason, greatly saddened me. Without knowing why, I was uncomfortable at her presence and I did not like her even before I had seen her.

Lucette arrived the day before she was expected. She was a big girl around nineteen or twenty with an opulent bosom, extremely white skin, a good but not unusual figure, a pretty mouth with carmine lips, and two perfect rows of enamel teeth. Immediately my preconception of her was changed. In addition, she had an excellent character, an abundance of gentleness and kindness, and a winning way. I was completely taken by her, and we soon became the most intimate friends. It was evident that my father was more than satisfied with her.

Envy and jealousy are strangers to my soul. Besides, what arouses the desire of men often is not our beauty or our merit. Thus, for the sake of our own happiness, it is wisest to let them alone and not to worry. More often than not their infidelity is nothing more than a slight fire that goes out as soon as it is lit. Consequently, it is folly to torment oneself about it.

Although I was not yet capable of reasoning in such a way at that time, I still felt no animosity towards Lucette. Besides, there was no diminishment in the signs of affection that my father bestowed on me. The only thing I perceived was his reserve when she was present but I put this down to mere shyness. Some weeks passed in this fashion until I finally noticed the attentions he was paying her. He never let an opportunity escape to reveal his feelings towards her. It was not long before I shared his sentiments for her.

When Lucette expressed her desire to sleep in my room, my father readily gave his consent. When he awoke in the morning, the first thing he did was to enter our chamber in which our beds were side to side. This arrangement enabled him to make advances towards Lucette while pretending that he had come to see me.

It was obvious that she was not rebuffing him, but she did not respond to his urgings as quickly as I would have liked her to, and I could not figure out the reason for her dragging feet. Loving my father as much as I did, I was of the opinion that everybody should feel towards him as I did. I could not help but chide her for her indifference.

'Why don't you like my Papa?' I asked her one day. 'He seems to have such warm feelings for you. I think that you are very ungrateful.'

She merely smiled at these reproaches, assuring me that I was doing her an injustice. She was right, for in a short time the apparent coolness vanished.

One evening after supper, we retired to a salon where my father had coffee and liqueurs served. In less than half an hour, Lucette was sound asleep. At that, my father took me up in his arms and carried me to my room where he put me to bed. Surprised at this new arrangement, my curiosity was instantly aroused. I got up a few moments later and tip-toed to the glass door, whose velvet curtain I slightly pushed aside so that I could look into the salon.

I was astonished to see Lucette's bosom completely uncovered. What charming breasts she possessed! They were two hemispheres as white as snow and firm as marble in the centre of which rose two little strawberries. The only movement they showed was from her regular breathing. My father was fondling them, kissing them and sucking them. In spite of his actions, she continued slumbering. Soon he began to remove all of her clothing, placing it on the edge of the bed. When he took off her shift, I saw two plump, rounded thighs of alabaster which he spread apart.

Then I made out a little vermilion slit adorned with a chestnut-brown tuft of hair. This he half opened, inserting his fingers which he vigorously manipulated in and out. Nothing roused her out of her lethargy.

Excited by the sight and instructed by the example, I imitated on myself the movements I saw and experienced sensations hitherto unknown to me. Laying her on the bed, my father came to the glass door to close it. I saved myself by hastening to the couch on which he had placed me. As soon as I was stretched out on the sheets, I began my rubbing, pondering what I had just viewed and profiting from what I had learned. I was on fire. The sensation I was undergoing increased in intensity, reaching such a height that it seemed my entire body and soul were concentrated in that one spot. Finally, I sank back in a state of exhausted ecstasy that enchanted me.

Returning to my senses, I was astonished to find myself almost soaked between my thighs. At first, I was very worried, but this anxiety was dispelled by the remembrance of the bliss I had just enjoyed. I fell into a deep sleep filled with dreams of my father caressing me. I was not yet awake when he came the next morning to awaken me with kisses which I eagerly returned.

Since that day, my governess and he seemed to have a secret understanding, although in the morning he did not remain with us as he formerly did. Of course, they had not the slightest suspicion that I was *au courant* as to what was going on, and lulled into a false security, during the day, they shamelessly flirted before retiring to my father's room where they remained for long periods of time.

With justice, I imagined that they were going to repeat what I had already seen, and my ideas did not go any further than that. Nevertheless, I was dying to view the same spectacle again. The reader can picture to himself the violent desire that was tormenting me. Finally came the moment when I was to learn everything.

Three days after the event I have just described, I took advantage of my father's absence to satisfy my burning curiosity. While Lucette was engaged in some task in another part of the house, I punctured a little hole in the silken curtain of the glass door.

I had not long to wait to profit from my stratagem. On my father's return, he immediately donned a flimsy dressing-gown and led to his room Lucette, who was in equally casual attire. They were careful to close the door and draw the curtain, but my preparations frustrated their precautions, at least in part. As soon as they were in the room, I was at the door with my face glued to the glass by the lifted curtain. The first person to meet my eyes was Lucette with her magnificent bosom completely bare. It was so seductive that I could not blame my father for immediately covering it with quick, eager kisses. Unable to hold himself back he tore off her clothing, and in a twinkling of the eye, skirt, corset and chemise were on the floor. How temptingly lovely she was in her natural state! I could not tear my eyes from her. She possessed all the charms and freshness of youth. Feminine beauty has a singular power and attraction for those of the same sex. My arms yearned to embrace those divine contours.

My father was soon in a state similar to his partner's. My eyes were fixed on him, because I had never seen him that way before. Now he placed her on the divan, which I could not see from my observation post.

Devoured by curiosity, I threw caution to the winds. I lifted the curtain until I could see everything. Not a detail escaped my eyes, and they spared themselves not the slightest voluptuousness.

I was able to perceive clearly Lucette stretched out on the couch and her fully expanded slit between the two chubby eminences. My father displayed a veritable jewel, a big member, stiff, surrounded by hair at the root below which dangled two balls. The tip was a scarlet red. I saw it enter Lucette's slit, lose itself there, and then reappear. This in-and-out movement continued for some time. From the fiery kisses they exchanged, I surmised that they were in raptures. Finally, I noticed the organ completely emerge. From the carmine tip which was all wet spurted a white fluid on Lucette's flat belly.

How the sight aroused me! I was so excited and carried away by desires I had not yet known that I attempted, at least partially, to participate in their delirium.

So entranced was I by the tableau that I remained too long and my imprudence betrayed me. My father, who had been too preoccupied with Lucette, now, disengaging himself from Lucette's arms, saw the partially lifted curtain. On spotting me, he wrapped himself in his robe as he approached the door. I hastily withdrew, but he raised the drape and discovered me trying to beat a retreat.

He stationed himself at the door while Lucette was

dressing. Seeing that he remained motionless, I fancied that he had not noticed anything. Still curious to know what was going on, I returned to the curtain. My astonishment when I met his face on the other side can be imagined. I was thunderstruck with fright.

By this time, Lucette had her clothes back on. My father pretended that nothing was amiss. Reminding Lucette of certain errands she had to carry out, he dismissed her, and I was alone with him.

When he came up to me, I was trembling and pale with fear. But, to my great surprise, instead of castigating me, he took me in his arms and covered me with a hundred kisses.

'Calm yourself, my dear Laurette,' he comforted me. 'Who in the world could have inspired the terror I see in your eyes? You need have no fear, my darling. You know that I have never harmed you. All I ask of you now is the truth. At this moment, I want you to consider me a friend rather than your father. Laura, I am your friend, and I beseech you to be sincere with me. Don't conceal anything from me. Tell me what you were doing when I was with Lucette and the reason for your peeking around this curtain. If you are honest, you will not have any reason to repent. If you aren't, my warm feelings for you will vanish and you can count on the convent.'

The mere mention of the final word had always filled me with dread. What I had heard of the life in those retreats! I mentally contrasted life there to that with my father. Besides, I had no doubt that I had witnessed everything. Finally, from past experience, I knew the wisdom of avowing everything to him, and I blurted out the entire truth.

Each detail I told him and each tableau I retraced, far from igniting his wrath, was repaid with kisses and caresses. I hesitated, nevertheless, at confessing the new, delicious experiences I had procured by myself, but he suspected them.

'Darling Laurette, you still haven't told me all,' he remarked, as he passed his hands over my derriere and kissed me. 'You should not hide anything from me. Give me the whole story.'

With some reluctance, I admitted that I had imitated his friction movements with Lucette, which had produced in me the most wonderful sensations. Even though I got all wet from doing it, I had repeated it three or four times, always with the same pleasure.

'But, dear Laura,' he cried, 'seeing what I put into Lucette, didn't you get the idea of inserting your finger into yourself?'

'No, Papa, the thought never crossed my mind.'

'Don't try to deceive me,' he warned. 'You can't hide anything from me. Come over here so I can see if you are telling the truth.'

'Honestly, Papa, I have told you the truth,' I protested.

Using the most endearing words with me, he led me into his bedroom, where he stretched me out on a couch. He lifted up my skirt and examined me carefully. Then, slightly opening my narrow slit, he tried to penetrate it with his little finger. The screams from the pain he was causing me made him stop.

'It is all inflamed, my child. Nevertheless, I recognize that you have not lied to me. The redness undoubtedly is due to the friction you committed on yourself while I was with Lucette.'

Now that I had lost my fear, I even told him that I could not obtain the pleasure I was looking for. The sincerity of my mouth was rewarded by a kiss from his. Then he lowered it, and with his tongue, tickled a certain spot that made me squeal with delight. I found this kind of caress new and heavenly. To bring my raptures to a peak he produced that member I had seen before. Involuntarily, I took it with one hand, while with the other, I opened his robe. He made no objection. I regarded with admiration and fondled that joyous instrument that I had seen disappear into Lucette's interior. How pleasing and unusual it was! From the first moment I touched it, I instinctively realized that it was the originator of pleasure. It went up and down in rhythm with the movement of my hand, which covered and uncovered the skin of the tip. Imagine my surprise when, after several moments of this sport, I saw gush out the same fluid that had flooded Lucette's thighs. As the last drops oozed, I noticed that he was trembling all over. I was happy that I had given a pleasure which I partially shared.

When I released my sticky hand, he resumed his previous game with his tongue. I was dying of an ineffable bliss. I was suffocating, but he continued.

'Dear Papa, stop it!' I pleaded. 'I can't stand it any longer.'

I fainted in his arms.

From that time on, everything became clear to me. What I had guessed before became a certainty. It seemed that the instrument I was touching was the magic key to understanding. Because of that organ, my father became even dearer to me. And my sentiments for him were returned in like measure.

He led me back to my room, where my governess appeared a few moments later. I did not have the slightest idea of what he was about to say to her.

'Lucette, from now on it is senseless to watch our step with Laura, for she knows everything.'

Then he repeated to her everything I had related to him and showed her the curtain. She appeared very disturbed, but I threw my arms around her neck, and my embraces, along with the reasons I gave her, quickly dissipated the embarrassment she had evinced. Kissing us both, he told Lucette not to leave me out of her sight. He left, returning an hour later with a woman who, as soon as she was in the room, made me completely disrobe and took my measurements for a sort of garment, the form of use of which I could not guess.

When it came time to go to bed, my father put me in Lucette's bed, admonishing her to keep an eye on me. Once again he departed, only to return a few minutes later and crawl in the same bed with us. I was between the two of them. My father held me in a tight hug. Covering with his hand the space between my legs, he prevented me from putting mine at that spot. I took his instrument, which surprised me because it was so limp and moist. I had never seen it in this pitiable state, imagining that it was always swollen, stiff and erect. But in my hand it was no longer slow in regaining the condition in which I knew it.

Lucette, who perceived what we were doing, was shocked.

'What you are doing with Laurette is outrageous,' she reproved him. 'Especially since you are her father.'

'You are partially right, Lucette,' he replied. 'But it is a secret that I wish to confide to you. It is to Laura's own interest that she keep her silence. Circumstances make it necessary that I tell you both.

'I had known her mother only fifteen days when I married her. The very first day after the wedding, I discovered her condition, but I considered it the wisest course to pretend not to notice it. In order that dates could not be put together, I took her to a distant province. After four months, Laura entered the world with all the vigour and health of a normal nine month infant. For six months more, I remained in that province, after which I brought the two back home. Now you recognize that this child who is so dear to me is not my own daughter in the strict sense of the word. Although she is not bound to me by flesh and blood, she is as dear to me as if she were.'

Then I immediately recalled the reply he had made to my mother's reproaches. The silence she maintained no longer appeared strange.

'But how could you have acted in such a way towards your wife?' Lucette wanted to know.

'Oh, I was never close to my wife,' my father nonchalantly answered. 'The Count de Norval, to whom Laura owes her entry into this life, is a likeable nobleman, a fine figure of a man with a handsome face, possessing those qualities that interest women. I wasn't the least bit surprised to learn that my wife had

27

succumbed to his attack. However, she was unable to marry him, for her parents did not find him wealthy enough for her. But if Laura is not my daughter by blood, the affection I have conceived for this adorable child renders her perhaps even more dear to me.

'Nevertheless, because of the mother's falsity I never approached her. I had an antipathy for her that I could not overcome. That is why I turned all my love to the innocent child.'

Lucette lavished on me hugs and kisses which told me that all her prejudices had been effaced. Warmly I returned her tokens of affection, even taking her enticing breasts and kissing and sucking the pink tips. My father stretched his hand to her and met mine, which he passed over Lucette's stomach and her thighs. Now my hand was guided over the fleece, the *mons Veneris*, and the crevice. I soon learned the names of all these portions of the female anatomy. Then I put my finger on the spot where I thought I would cause her pleasure. There I came across something rather hard and distended.

'Good, Laura!' my father complimented me. 'You are holding the most sensitive part. Move your hand without relinquishing the clitoris while I stick my finger in her little cunt.'

Lucette, her arm about me, caressing my buttocks, took my father's prick and introduced it between my thighs, but he did not put it in nor did he make the slightest movement. Soon my governess was at the peak of pleasure. Her kisses multiplied and her sighs became moans.

'Stop! That's enough!' she moaned. 'Faster! Put it

in all the way, my dearest. My God, I am coming! This is the end.'

How these expressions of voluptuousness delighted me. I felt that her cunt was all damp. My father's finger came out, all covered with what she had discharged. I was beside myself with excitement. Taking Lucette's hand, I brought it to between my legs so that she would do to me what I had done for her, but my father, covering my mound with his hand, stopped her. He was too much of a libertine not to be sparing of his pleasures, and he moderated his desires, leaving me up in the air by recommending us to calm ourselves. We fell asleep, our arms interlaced, plunged into the sweetest intoxication. I had never spent such a delicious night.

When the rays of the morning sun brought us back to life, Lucette and I looked at each other. Then I noticed a note pinned to the chair. It was from Papa who wrote that he would be away all day, but he knew that Lucette would take good care of me. Excitedly, I reminded my companion that it was the servants' day off and we would be alone. We beamed at each other with radiant smiles.

I nestled closer to her for I loved to sniff the sharp odour that came from her svelte body. I nuzzled my nose between her breasts to breathe it in more deeply. It reminded me of carrots, and every time I smelled it, I quivered with excitement.

'I think I am too fat,' she remarked. 'Don't you think so?'

She lifted up her nightgown as if to prove her point. I wondered why she thought she was so fat. Her legs were lovely and well-rounded, and her buttocks

dimpled and charming. There was not the trace of a
bulge on her body. The magnificent breasts were so
heavy that I wondered how they could jut out as they
did. And I could not keep my eyes from the clump of
luxuriant hair under her armpits. When she turned
her back to me, I saw her derriere, two superb hemispheres that must have been fashioned in heaven.

'You are not too plump,' I affirmed again. 'On the
contrary, it seems to me that you are just right.'

She gave me a pleased pout as she got out of bed
and walked to the desk with the cheeks of her bottom
swaying seductively from side to side. She returned to
the warm bed with a large album of art reproductions,
many of them of nude women and in co!˙ur.

'Look,' she said, pointing out one to me. 'She is far
more slender than I.'

'Yes, but on the other hand, this woman by Rubens
is far plumper than you.'

'That may be so, but I still should lose some weight.
A massage does the trick, and you can help me if you
wish.'

'I? . . . Massage you? I have never done that
before. . . .'

'There's nothing difficult about it. It's just the sort
of favour one does for a friend. And you are my friend,
aren't you?'

I puffed up with pride at that. But I felt a certain
uneasiness not unmingled with anticipation.

'And I have just the thing for a massage,' she added
with a slight blush.

'What do you mean by that?' I asked her in some
puzzlement. 'I always thought you massaged with the
hands.'

'There are also appliances that are helpful in removing excess flesh. . . . I'll get mine.'

She went to her room and came back with a rubber glove covered with bumps. It reminded me of the skin of a toad. Lucette ran it up and down my arm. It gave me goose-pimples but the sensation was not unpleasant.

'How do you like it, Laura?' she asked with a glint in her eyes.

Then she applied it on her shoulders, her arms and above her breasts. I felt a twinge of envy.

'I hope I'll be able to use it correctly and not hurt you. I have never seen anything like that before. If I am clumsy, please forgive me.'

'There's no danger, but I'll have to lie down.'

Now she was on her stomach, lovelier than ever, particularly since her lush body was reflected in the wall mirror.

'Now start at the top of my back,' she ordered.

This promised to be fun. The skin quivered and turned pink where I touched it with my gloved hand. Lucette remained motionless, her head between her arms and her hair over her ears. After vigorously treating the glorious buttocks, she suddenly turned over.

'And now the breasts, Laura.'

Nervously, I did as I was bid. The gorgeous globes shivered as much as my hand. Taking my hand, she made it descend to one of the rosy nipples.

'Look,' she said.

To my astonishment, I saw it dilate, swell, get hard and jut out. It became a crimson mountain peak. Then she made me put it on the other. As I rubbed

31

the mound, there occurred, to my uneasiness, the same phenomenon.

'I'm in heaven,' Lucette blissfully sighed. 'That's the way nipples become when they are handled that way. Now the belly, Laura, and the hips. It is so wonderful when you do it, and I can't tell you how grateful I am.'

My eyes were glued to the hard breasts, the hollow navel, and the dark triangle whose hair extended almost all the way up to her waist. Mentally, I compared myself with her. I had only a pitiful little fleece there, while hers was a carpet, a beautiful luxurious Persian rug.

I revolved the glove on her stomach around her navel. I did not dare get too close to the triangle, for I was afraid that it might get tangled in the matted hair and hurt her. She was lasciviously wiggling her hips with her eyes shut. It was obvious that she was in an incipient ecstasy. Her toes contracted and sometimes her knee twitched when I got too close to the erogenous zone.

'Now between the thighs,' she murmured without opening her eyes. I observed that her nipples were straining more than ever.

Reassured that I was giving her pleasure, I redoubled my efforts as I rubbed the glove on the silky skin. But I could not keep my eyes from the luxuriant thicket. I wondered how what it was concealing would look like.

I was sure that mine would be put to shame in comparison.

The more I kept at it, the more pleasure it gave me. I was not a little disappointed when she told me to stop. Reading my feelings in my face, Lucette laughed.

'I can see that you are unwilling to give up, dearest Laura,' she said. 'But don't be disappointed, I need a bit of a breathing spell, for that puts my nerves on edge. Why, you are perspiring! Take off your nightgown. You'll be much more comfortable. I don't think you are bashful after last night.'

'A little,' I confessed, but I followed her suggestion.

'Completely nude, that's the way I want you,' she breathed. 'I adore nudity. I can never get enough of looking at myself naked in a mirror. I never feel alone when I can regard my reflection in the mirror. We were so excited last night that I did not notice what adorable little breasts you have. And what promise your delicate figure shows!'

The compliments gave me so much pleasure that I could not conceal my blushes. I wanted to bury my face in her arms. Hurling myself at her, I feverishly kissed her cheeks. She looked at me straight in the eyes, holding my gloved hands in hers.

'Continue,' she commanded.

Eagerly, too eagerly I resumed my task. She promptly rebuked me.

'Not so fast and not so hard,' she scolded. 'Just run it gently over my whole body. Do you understand?'

Now I did not press down so hard. Lucette closed her eyes in contentment.

'It's like a lover's caress,' she murmured.

In the mirror I could see the bed, the naked body of my new friend, and mine which was trembling and twitching. At the same time, I regarded my little, rounded, apple-like breasts with their tawny tips, and

33

came to the conclusion that I was not too bad. Perhaps I was not as abundant as Lucette, but I was not her inferior. My charms were just on a smaller scale.

Now her mouth was agape and her breathing laboured. I twisted the glove on her stomach and breasts. Each time I touched a nipple, she gave a start, convulsively lifted a knee, and spread her legs. When I took the rubber glove away, she became motionless.

'Farther down, Laura,' she whispered as if I were neglecting her spread thighs. I massaged the inside of them. From the knees, the glove gradually ascended to the groin and the buttocks.

It was then that I noticed a curious movement of her pelvis. She kept lifting and dropping it in fits and starts. At the same time, she was rattling in her throat and trying to catch her breath.

Going up still farther, I put the glove on the hairs of her mound. Her jerky movements became more agitated and vehement. Suddenly, she grasped my hand and spread her legs as far apart as she could.

'There . . . there!' she panted. 'Don't take it away. Keep it where it is. How good it feels!'

I was a little afraid at the way she was flopping about. Her legs shot up in the air and then limply dropped. I watched her face. It was livid, contorted in a grimace that deformed her features. Horrified, I tried to take away the glove, but she held it firmly in position. I wondered what was wrong with her. After more convulsions, both her body and face relaxed. For several minutes she remained without life or movement.

When I took off the glove, wondering if I had hurt her with it, she opened her eyes and smiled sweetly at me.

'It was sheer bliss,' she said dreamily.

I was dumbfounded. How could she say a thing like that when I had seen how she was suffering?

'You don't understand, I see,' she told me. 'And I can't explain. It is something that you have to experience yourself. Do you want me to massage you in turn?'

'But won't it hurt?' I timidly asked. 'You were groaning and moaning so, and the words you said, I was really afraid.'

'Do you love me that much, Laura?'

'Yes, yes, I love you . . . more than anything.'

In such gambols we spent the day and night.

When Lucette and I awoke, we were still locked in each other's arms. My father entered, bringing with him the woman who had come the previous day. My surprise and chagrin were great when she put on me morocco leather shorts which descended from my hips to slightly above my knees. They were loosely fitting and not constraining at all. The girdle fitted me perfectly around the waist and two straps holding up the shorts passed over my shoulders. They could be loosened or tightened at will. The girdle had an opening in the front that extended four inches down. Along this aperture, there were eyelets on both sides through which my father passed a little chain of delicately worked silver gilt which he locked with a little key.

'My dear Laura, adorable child, I am greatly concerned about your health and your preservation.

Chance has instructed you already in that which should only have learned at the age of eighteen. Consequently, I have to take precautions against your premature knowledge and the inclinations you have by nature and love. In time, you'll come to share my judgment, but nothing you will say now will change my mind.'

At first I was infuriated, and I could not conceal my ill temper, but on reflection I realized the gratitude I owed my father.

He had foreseen everything. At the bottom of these shorts was a little silver gondola the size of the space between my thighs. In this my little mound was completely encased, while on either side it covered my little cunt and my asshole. It was not uncomfortable. It was so fashioned that I could perform my natural functions without any inconvenience, but it was impossible to insert my finger into the narrow aperture to masturbate, which was what my father desired to prevent above all things.

Since that time, I have often seen such contraptions on boys to keep them from wasting their virility before their time, for no matter how one keeps an eye on them, they go their own awkward way, much to their regret in later years.

For two years, my father removed the shorts every evening, which Lucette cleaned after washing me. After ascertaining that the chastity contrivance was not hurting me, he put it back on. From that day until I was eighteen, I had to wear the thing night and day. But during that period I learned a great deal, for I was curious by nature. Each year saw my knowledge increase, and I was indefatigable in my studies.

I had become used to my imprisonment, and the thought that one day I would be rid of it made it bearable.

Among the questions I most frequently asked him was the reason for my restraint and what were the precautions he was taking with regard to me, for he kept postponing my freedom until I was older. It was on my eighteenth birthday that he finally satisfied my curiosity.

'Now I think it is about time, dear Papa, for you to tell my why I have to wear this horrible thing, especially since you keep telling me how much you love me. Lucette is happier than I, and surely you care for her less than you do for me. I insist on knowing why you have done this to me.'

With that, I stamped my foot and shook my curls in determination.

'I have to agree that you are no longer a child, and it is time that I should give you an explanation. With men, nature starts to manifest itself around the age of fifteen or sixteen, but it reaches its peak at seventeen or eighteen. When one diverts its operations by premature and numerous discharges, so that this development is weakened, the results are felt for the rest of one's life.

'It is the same with women. If they waste their resources at too early an age, they will die early, become enfeebled and languid, and suffer from depression. They become so thin that they fall easy prey to tuberculosis. As a result, they are not able to enjoy the sweetest pleasure life has to offer.

37

'Because of my deep and tender love for you, dearest Laurette, I wanted to keep you from such a terrible fate, and what I did to you was for your own good.'

Although I had a deep-seated penchant for pleasure and voluptuousness, I had no desire to obtain them at such a price, and the prospect, as painted by my father, frightened me.

'I recognized such inclinations in you,' my father continued, 'and I knew that reason would have no power against your innate sensuousness. That is why I wanted to protect you against yourself, and I have to tell you that it is not yet time to set you free, for there are still many dangers lurking which you cannot cope with now.'

The thought of impaired health and the fear of an early death were vivid in my imagination. Nevertheless, what I had seen him do with Lucette and the way he lived with her weakened somewhat the impact of his dire predictions. I could not help but express to him my doubts.

'Why don't you take the same precautions with Lucette as you do with me, Papa? Why do you give her so often what you absolutely forbid me?'

'Why, my daughter,' he replied, 'Lucette is a fully formed woman. Besides, if she retains within her too much fluid of life, it would ravage her health by stagnating. Moreover, it would hinder the circulation of her blood. When that happens, a woman becomes dizzy, demented, exhausted and delirious. You can see horrible examples in certain nunneries where the sisters are so closely watched that they have no outlets for their natural desires. Remedies have been attempted, but the results have been worse than the cure.

'With some women, the ardour of temperament is quenched earlier than with others, and I want yours to continue as long as possible. When the time is right, you will have no cause to repent of your long continence and you will receive the life-giving fluid as copiously as Lucette does. Now you can understand my behaviour towards you.'

'Papa, for that is how I shall always call you,' I protested, 'I can understand your reasoning, but how long do I have to wait until you do with me what you do with her? I can hardly wait for that moment, since I am so eager to satisfy your desires to the fullest extent.'

'Wait until nature speaks more loudly,' he counselled me. 'Wait just a little longer when you will have the force. Then, Laurette, I shall receive the full measure of tenderness you have for me. You will allow me to pluck that rare blossom that I have been so carefully cultivating, but that moment has not yet come.'

His words were etched in my memory, and his reasoning seemed based on such a sound foundation, his readiness to answer my questions openly prompted me to query him further. I had always wondered about Lucette, who was in such a profound sleep the first time I found them together. To me, it was a mystery that I wanted cleared up. Finally, one day, I asked him.

'Papa, why was Lucette sleeping so soundly the first day you bared her breasts and why didn't she wake up while you were doing everything you wanted with her? Was she really asleep or was she just pretending?'

'She was really asleep,' he replied. 'It is a secret, but I am going to let you in on it, for it will be a lesson to you. I'll admit that for some time I was torn with desire. I became excited with you, but you could afford me no satisfaction. I liked Lucette at first sight, and I found her agreeable in every way. But seeing that she was hesitant about giving in to me, I determined on a bold step. I put some sleeping powder in the glass of liqueur that I offered her. You saw the effect. But I was not satisfied with that. I was afraid that if she woke up, surprise and anger would ruin all my plans. In order to prevent that, I had prepared in advance a potion designed to arouse all her sensuousness. That is what is called a love philtre. After I had put you in my bed, I went back to get several drops which I rubbed on her mound, her clitoris and her lips. This liquid has the power to excite even the most enfeebled and give him an erection if he smears it on his organ shortly before he enters combat.

'Lucette had not been asleep an hour before she awoke, feeling an itching, a burning, and a passion which nothing could extinguish. She did not seem surprised to see me in her arms, for she passed hers around my neck. Far from opposing my caresses and desires, for she herself was deeply moved, she voluntarily spread her legs wide. It was a matter of seconds before I was revelling in the most exquisite delights that I made her share. I was attentive to the consequences that could ensue, for at the moment when I sensed rapture ready to shoot out like a flame, I withdrew, inundating her mound and belly with a copious libation, an offering to the altar at which I was then worshipping.

'From that time, Lucette has always lent herself to my desires. It was because of her complacency, my inattention, and the curiosity I did not suspect in one your age that you discovered our secret. She does not know what I have just taught you, and you must keep my confidence.'

'You need have no worry on that score, dear Papa,' I assured him. 'But please finish your story. Aren't you afraid of getting her with child if you don't always pull out in time? Are you always in control of yourself? Aren't you sometimes carried away by ecstasy? And the fear that one has for the consequences, doesn't that diminish the pleasure?'

'Ah, my dear child,' he sighed, 'where your imagination doesn't take you! I recognize fully that I should not conceal anything from you. I don't run any risk with you, for you are intelligent beyond your years.'

'First of all, semen which is not shot into the matrix bears no fruit. There are ways to prevent it from reaching its goal, but you will learn about this when you are older. I use an infallible method with Lucette which enables her to give herself up to her passions without any worry. Before we start our lovemaking, she fits herself out with a special device which makes it impossible for her to produce children.'

I nodded in understanding.

Such were some of the conversations we had, mostly for my benefit. It goes without saying that they were frequently interrupted by kisses and caresses. Libertine books of all kinds were freely placed in my hands for me to peruse, but those that pertained to my sex

41

were stressed. We discussed religion, and according to my father, God is 'incomprehensible; he is felt rather than known. He demands our respect and despises our speculations.' My father reduced morality to, 'Do unto others as you would have them do unto you,' or 'Do not do unto others what you would not have them do unto you.'

As I pursued these studies, my figure was filling out; my pointed breasts had acquired an admirable amplitude. Every day I showed their progress to Lucette and my father, who gladly kissed them at my request. I put their hands on them to show them how firm and full they were. Finally, I made no secret of the fact that I was at the end of my patience. Never having had to curb my temper, I no longer listened to or followed anything but the voice of nature. I could see that this banter was arousing my father.

'You're getting an erection, dear Papa. Come over here,' I ordered, and placed him in Lucette's arms.

Although I was deeply aroused, I still found enjoyment in their pleasures. She and I lived in the closest intimacy; she cherished me as much as I loved her. I slept ordinarily with her, and I never failed her when my father was absent. I fulfilled my role the best I could. While hugging her, I sucked her lips and the buttons of her Junoesque breasts, and I kissed the cheeks of her derriere and her smooth belly and her delicious *mons Veneris*. I stroked her entire body. Often my fingers took the place that I could not supply her with, and I plunged her into agonies of rapture which was a delight to see. My good will and complaisance caused her to feel for me an affection that is impossible to describe. During our lovemaking, many times she.

had noticed me violently animated and she assured me that she ardently desired to procure for me the same ecstasies I was giving her.

'Yes, my dear Laura,' she breathed, 'when the great moment arrives, I plan on having a grand celebration. I can't wait for it. I have the feeling that the time is not far off. Your delightful breasts are just about perfectly rounded. Your arms and legs are shapely and your mound, already covered with a soft fleece, is rising. Your pretty little cunt is now a rosy pink. In your eyes, I see that something which puts you in the ranks of womanhood. Last spring, you saw some preludes of eruptions which are going to be a fact very quickly.'

Indeed, in a short time I felt more sluggish, my head was heavy, my eyes lustreless; I had pains in my back and attacks of colic. After eight days of this, Lucette found the gondola covered with blood. My father, on seeing this, did not put it back on me, for they had foreseen this. I was told of my situation. For about a week, I remained almost in a stupor, after which I was as gay and full of health as I had been before.

My happiness at my newfound freedom was indescribable. I was beside myself with joy as I threw my arms around Lucette's neck.

'How happy I am going to be!' I cried.

Then I ran to my father, whom I likewise embraced, and exultantly told him: 'Here I am in the state in which you desire me. How happy I shall be if I can arouse your desires and satisfy them! My bliss is to belong entirely to you. My love and tenderness are the goal of my felicity.'

Taking me in his arms, he sat me on his knees. With

what passion he returned the embraces I bestowed on him. He squeezed and kissed my woman's breasts; he sucked my lips; his tongue sought mine; and my buttocks and my cunt were both victims of his feverish hands.

'The moment has finally come, dearest Laurette,' he panted, 'this blessed instant when your tenderness and mine are going to be united in the breast of voluptuousness. I want to have your maidenhead this very day, to pluck the flower that has just blossomed. I owe it to your love, and your sentiments towards me put an inestimable value on the offering you are about to make. But I should warn you that if ineffable bliss follows our embraces and kisses, the moment when I become master of that charming rosebud, you will be pricked by some thorns that will cause you pain.'

'What does it matter?' I exclaimed. 'Make me suffer. Slash me until I bleed if you wish. I cannot make enough sacrifices for you. Your pleasure and your satisfaction are the sole object of my desires.'

My eyes were sparkling. The ever-helpful Lucette, wishing to cooperate in the bloodletting of the victim, showed herself as eager as if she had been herself the executioner. They lifted me up and carried me into a chamber that they had prepared for the time when I would be ready. The light of day was completely banished from it. In a recess surrounded by mirrors was a bed covered with a blue satin covering, and on it was a cushion of fire-red silk which was to be the sacrificial altar.

Quickly, Lucette exposed all the charms nature had bestowed on me. I, the sacrifice, was adorned only with crimson ribbons which she knotted above my elbows and waist. I resembled another Venus. Another ribbon was woven in my loose hair. Without any hesitation, I threw myself on the couch.

Regarding myself in the mirrors, I found myself more beautiful than I would be had I been wearing any ornaments. I felt very satisfied with myself. My skin was of a dazzling whiteness; my little but firm pink nipples rose proudly from the enticing breasts; a delicate fleece shaded the plump little mound, which, slightly open, revealed a clitoris stuck out from between two lips called pleasure and voluptuousness. Add to that a svelte, shapely figure, slender legs ending in dainty feet, buttocks like little apples, and a small of the back with all the freshness of Hebe. If I had been competing against the three goddesses, Paris certainly would have bestowed the apple of victory on me. Such was the praise that Lucette and my father vied in heaping on me. I was bursting with pride. The more I thought myself lovely, the more they encouraged me in the belief. My father in particular could not get over my charms. He examined and admired me. His hands and ardent lips were all over my body. We were like two young lovers who up until now had met only with difficulty and who were going to get recompense for their patience and affection.

I so wanted to see him in the state I was. At my insistence, he quickly ripped off his clothing with the assistance of Lucette. He arranged me on the bed so that my derriere was on the cushion. In my hand I held the sacred blade that in an instant was to immolate my virginity. This prick that I was passionately caressing was of a stiffness to prove to me that it would surely pierce the rose that he had so carefully tended for such a long time. My imagination was burning with desire. My cunt was on fire and calling for that dear prick which I immediately set on its path.

We were locked in each other's arms, glued to each other. Our mouths and tongues devoured one another. I noticed that he was holding himself back, but passing my legs over his rump and squeezing as hard as I could, I gave an upward thrust with my backside so that he went in as far as he could go. The pain I felt and the scream that escaped from my lips were signs of his victory.

Inserting her hand between us, Lucette stroked my cunt and with the other hand tickled my asshole. The melange of pain and pleasure, and the flowing fuck and blood raised me to paradise, to an ineffable sensuousness.

I was suffocating; I was expiring. My arms and legs became limp and my head sagged. I was no longer among the living. But I took a delectation in these excesses that I could barely stand. What an exquisite state! Soon I was roused from my sweet lethargy by renewed caresses. He kissed me, sucked me, and massaged my breasts, the cheeks of my derriere, and my mount. He lifted my legs into the air to have the pleasure of regarding from a different angle my backside, my cunt and the ravages he had committed. His prick that I was still clutching and his testicles which Lucette was stroking were soon restored to their former rigidity. The former he quickly inserted into me. Now that the passage had been made easier, his penetration was nothing but sheer joy. Goodhearted Lucette renewed her titillations, and I again fell back into the lascivious apathy I had just experienced.

My father, proud of his triumph and delighted at the willingness with which I had succumbed, took the bloodstained cushion that was under me and embraced it as the trophy of his victory.

'Dear Laura,' he said as he tenderly lay down on the pillow, 'good Lucette has multiplied your pleasures. Don't you think it would be the right thing to do to let her join in our frolics?'

I threw my arms around her neck and pulled her down with me on the bed, where I lifted up her skirt and found her all damp.

'How aroused you must have been,' I said understandingly. 'Now I wish to give you at least a portion of the bliss I have just enjoyed.'

Taking my father's hand, I introduced one finger into her and he pushed it in and out while I caressed her. It was a matter of instants before she was in that state of ecstasy from which I had just emerged.

By now, we were soaked in sweat, and Papa suggested we all take a bath together. Lucette and I enthusiastically agreed. The three of us rushed to the large tub which Papa had foresightedly filled with lukewarm water beforehand. Papa and Lucette were the first to get in and then I. Being the youngest, it was I who soaped them down. Papa complimented me on my enthusiasm for my task, which I did not find irksome in the least. I paid special attention to the opulent breasts and Junoesque derriere of my governess and the shaggy hair on the chest and at the bottom of the stomach of my supposed sire. His sex was the particular object of my care. As a joke, I inserted the bar of soap into Lucette's slit. This caused general merriment.

After I bestowed a filial kiss on Papa's virility, it was my turn to receive their attention. First smearing me from chin to knees, he started a systematic fondling to which I reacted with ardour. Then we rinsed ourselves with fresh water to get rid of the mucous irritations caused by the soap. Once we were dried, Papa felt in a jovial mood.

'Lucette, let's show little Laura some games she has not seen.'

'Oh yes, let's,' Lucette cried, clapping her hands. 'But Laura has to help.'

'Indeed she does.'

Papa sat on the bidet, which I was ordered to fill with water up to the brim. His testicles and backside were completely wetted. Then I had to sit behind him with my arms around his waist. Under Lucette's guidance, my right hand began to stroke his masculinity while the left squeezed and released the testicles. Finally, my finger was led into his rear aperture. He gave a start and squeal of joy.

Lucette went back into the bedroom and returned with two thick books which she placed before Papa's feet, one on each side of the bidet. Then she stepped on them, placing her hands on his shoulders. In this position, the matted shaggy mound, already moist with desire, was directly in front of his face. Without hesitation, he darted his tongue into the inviting grotto. For better penetration, he firmly clutched the two callipygian hemispheres of his lovely Lucette.

Releasing one of them, he dipped his finger into the vagina which he vigorously stirred.

Now the only sounds heard were the grunts of the lovers and the slipslop of Papa's tongue lapping the vulva and the clitoris to the tempo of my hands fondling his sex and swollen sacks. So that I could take part in the sport, Papa withdrew his hand from Lucette and began to titillate my excited inflamed button.

It was Papa who reached bliss first. His initial jet was so powerful that it splattered the wall and drenched Lucette's thighs. The succeeding spurts plopped into the bidet water like hail stones on a pond. The sound triggered Lucette and myself to release our fluids, which we did with long lingering sighs.

We were so exhausted that some repose was necessary. Lucette and Papa were soon dozing in the bed, while I went to my room. When I came back, I saw that they were just awakening. I hid behind the curtain. Lucette was smiling affectionately at Papa and her affectionate embraces soon produced another erection. At the sight of the angry organ, she felt overwhelming desire. With a jerk of her powerful derriere, she threw off the sheets and blankets, pressed her fleshy lips on the hirsute torso, nibbling the nipples, and slid her mouth down to the navel. One of her hands blindly clutched the pulsating virility. Getting off the bed and kneeling on the rug, she thrust her head between Papa's dangling legs.

When Papa espied me, I gave a little cry of surprise, covered my eyes with my hands, and taking off my shift, clambered into the bed with Papa. I shoved a pillow under his head and put my thighs over him. I dug my hands into his wavy hair.

Papa was unable to resist the temptation of the delicious slit, which I had slightly perfumed, right in front of his nose. As his tongue automatically thrust itself into it, I gave a shriek of delight and squeezed his head tightly between my two legs. I was beside myself with pleasure at the cadence of his tongue which I regulated with the up-and-down movement of my pelvis. I took particular joy in rubbing my irritated clitoris on his nose.

Abandoning her fellation, Lucette got up and bestrode Papa on the edge of the bed. This change of position somewhat cooled Papa's ardour, for he was on the verge of ejaculating in Lucette's mouth if only she had continued her oral activity. After several downward thrusts, she was unable to hold back her orgasm and collapsed on my shoulders, gasping with pleasure. At that, I went into an almost uncontrollable spasm and gushed my inner glycerine into Papa's mouth.

Breathless, Lucette and I fell back in a near faint. Of the three of us, Papa was the only one who felt cheated, and he demanded recompense. He nodded at Lucette, who shook her head in refusal. There was only myself left, but I could see that he was reluctant to re-enter my cunt, still tight and narrow in spite of my recent defloration. But he began to caress the labia and tickle the clitoris. He whispered a few words into Lucette's ear.

She promptly stretched out on the sheets and ordered me to get on top of her, back to belly. Then Lucette put her legs on mine, spreading her knees as far apart as she could. With this manoeuvre, she so widened my cunt that the interior gaped open. It was now child's play for Papa to insert his weapon into the still damp aperture.

I was delighted and more than ready for another bout. But still the memory of the first pain caused me worry. But like a skilled tactician, Papa launched a surprise attack. His first rhythmic thrusts were barely perceptible. It seemed that the hymen had again erected its barrier. He stopped for several seconds before starting again his methodical boring, gradually gaining a few centimetres at a time. When I relaxed, he pursued his advantage to win a little more ground. Now he was at the halfway mark with another victory in sight if he did not make a misstep.

Now he employed another method of ingress, this time a corkscrew movement. In my delirium, I could see the expression of triumph on his face when he felt that it was succeeding.

Success crowned his efforts. The fleshy sword was in to the bottom of me, in spite of the narrowness of the contested valley.

I was groaning with a pleasure I had never before experienced – the first time the pain had blunted the bliss – and marvelling at the sensation in the depths of my stomach. It was a victory that Papa could well be proud of. The look on his face seemed to say: 'Ah, my little one. I finally got you. You got me to stick my tongue in your cunt, but in turn you got a prick that is going to give you a squirt you'll never forget.'

I was conquered.

I was dripping wet inside and it eased the action of his piston. Now he went at his work in a rage. His belly slapped the victim's with every jab. Sensing the approach of the supreme moment, Lucette released my lips and inserted her finger to Papa's slimy rear hole.

The reaction was immediate. In a roar of triumph and voluptuousness, Papa stopped his frenzied injections and stiffened as he shot the hot jets of his sperm into the ecstatic womb which answered his stream with one of hers.

Ah, how many charms that day held for me! It was the most wonderful one in all my life and the first in which I savoured the delights of sensuousness to the full. This memory which causes me so much pleasure brings at the same time the bitterest regrets. But I want to forget about that for the time being.

There reigned in the room an agreeable sultriness, and I was so comfortable the way I was that I did not want to put anything on. I was in such a gay mood that I wanted to have supper naked. Lucette, always on the alert, had had the good sense to dismiss all the servants, and she prepared the meal herself after locking all the doors. Still I was not satisfied. I wanted her to be as we were, and without further ado, I tore off her few garments. She made an enchanting picture. Thus we sat at the table. Seated between the two of us, my father was the object of our fondlings which he gave back in good measure. The mirrors multiplied the charm of the tableau we formed. Our moods and attitudes were varied by our sallies inspired by a delicate wine.

Under its influence our cunts became inflamed and Papa's prick resumed its old stiffness and firmness. In the state of mind we were in, the table no longer pleased us and we hurried back to the bed. During that day, which was consecrated to me, I was plunged once again into the delights of supreme voluptuousness. Papa lay on my left, his legs under my raised ones, and his prick proudly presented itself to the entrance.

Lucette stretched herself out on me, my head between her knees. Her delightful little cunt was just above my eyes; I half-opened it and tickled it while I stroked her buttocks which were stuck up in the air. Her stomach was grazing my breasts and her thighs were between my arms. All was calculated to ignite the flame of passion.

She spread wide the lips of my cunt which was now a deep red. I urged her to put the contraceptive into it so that my father could enjoy me and discharge into me without any worry.

My cunt hurt like anything, and the pain became even worse as soon as it was touched. In spite of this soreness, I endured the procedure with the knowledge that it would be succeeded by sensations more agreeable. Lucette conducted my father's prick onto the path from which she had removed all the dangers and which was now strewn only with flowers. He rushed along it, and quickly sank into the aperture. Her finger was also inside at the same time. I rendered her a similar service while my father was doing the same thing in her cunt with his finger that his prick was doing in mine.

These variations, these positions, and this multiplicity of personages and sensations in the preliminaries enhanced infinitely their delights. Simultaneously we felt them approaching, but ready to escape us like a flash of lightning, and we savoured them to their fullest extent. Now we began to feel fatigue. Lucette, who was the first to get up, set everything in order. As soon as she was back, we returned to the bed and, wrapped in one another's arms, fell back to sleep.

My disappointment that such joys were not to be had every day can be imagined. My father, always solicitous about the state of my health, ordered me back into the chastity belt.

'My dear Laurette,' he explained to me, 'I do not hide from you that I have misgivings about you and all of us. Your character is not yet sufficiently formed so that I can leave you to your own devices, and you are too dear to me for me not to guide your steps for a while longer. Nonetheless, you will have your pleasure from our lovemaking. You'll do it with us, and, in a certain manner, you will share our pleasure. Also, from time to time, we'll reserve for you a similar night, which you will find much more agreeable if you have to wait for it. Finally, if you wish to please me, you will lend yourself to what I desire of you, and you will comply without argument.'

That was his method of rendering my new imprisonment less unbearable.

Nineteen months had passed since that memorable evening when I learned to my sorrow that Lucette was leaving us. Her father, who lived in the provinces and was mortally ill, had summoned her for a last meeting. Her departure caused us the greatest regret. Our sincere tears mingled with hers. As for myself, I could not hold back my sobs, which finally subsided when she said she would return to us as quickly as she could. But shortly after the death of her father, she went into a decline from which it took two years for her to recover. Her father had left her a comfortable inheritance which made her much sought after by the young bachelors of the region, but she would have nothing to do with them. According to her letters, they formed such a contrast with my father that all those who paid her suit, she found absolutely revolting. Marriage was the furthest thing from her mind and her greatest wish was to return to us.

Nevertheless, urged by her mother and other relatives who praised the advantages to be found where she was, and the need that her infirm parent had of her, she was finally persuaded to remain with her family, much against her will, but only after consulting with my father in whom she had the greatest confidence.

Since the suitor who presented himself offered numerous advantages, my father felt himself obliged out of a sense of principle to advise her to accept him, a decision which he found extremely repugnant to make, for he confided in me several times that he had a presentiment of misfortune for her, but to which he could not lend credence, regarding it as a weakness. His foreboding was correct, however, for she died in her first childbirth.

Often I regretted the departure of Lucette, whose loss I regarded as my own, but I consoled myself in the arms of my dear and tender father. I had finally rid myself for good of that detestable attachment I had so often cursed. But what had happened to Lucette because of her excesses weighed heavily on me and made me realize how careful I would have to be because of my delicate constitution. I confided my misgivings to my father, with whom I slept every night. He was never far from me and he watched over me like a guardian angel, stopping me when I yielded to my desires with too much ardour.

After Lucette's departure, he had made some changes in his suite. For example, one could only enter my room by passing through his. Our beds touched against the same wall. Thus not even the servants had the slightest inkling of our frolics.

It was during one of those delightful nights that he enabled me to enjoy a new kind of pleasure, one of which I didn't have the slightest idea. It was marvellous.

'Dearest Laura,' he began. 'You have given me your first flower, but you possess another blossom that you owe me, one you cannot refuse me if you hold me dear.'

'Oh, Papa, you know the depth of my love for you,' I exclaimed. 'What do I have left that you want? Whatever it is, I give it to you with all my heart, and nothing would give me greater pleasure than for you to have it. Your happiness is my only goal.'

'Dear girl,' he replied, deeply moved. 'I am so delighted with you. Your generosity and nobility match your beauty and grace. The soul of voluptuousness resides in you. It presents itself in myriad forms on every part of your body. Your hands, mouth, armpits, breasts and derriere are all cunt.'

'Take your choice. You're the master, and I lend myself to your slightest desire,' I cried.

He made me turn on my left side with my buttocks

facing him. Moistening my asshole and the head of his prick, he inserted it, so very gently. The difficulty of the passage gave us nothing but a new path strewn with accumulated pleasures. Supporting my leg with his raised knee, he masturbated me, sticking his finger in my cunt from time to time. I was almost wild from this exhilaration on both sides. When he sensed that I was on the verge. he quickened his movements, which I seconded with mine. Then I felt the bottom of my backside inundated with a boiling fluid which produced, on my part, an abundant discharge. I relished an ineffable delight. It seemed as if all the parts of my body were fused into one spasm of lust. My convulsions and transports were all due to that incomparable sharp-pointed virility belonging to a man whom I adored.

'What a ravishing pleasure,' sighed my father. 'What do you have to say about it? Judging from your moans and movements, you must have enjoyed it as much as I.'

'Ah, Papa,' I breathed. 'It was infinite, new and strange. How can I put into words all the varied raptures I experienced? What happened before was as nothing to what I just now enjoyed.'

'In that case, my dear child, another time I will employ a dildo to give you new pleasures, ones that you never dreamed of.'

'Papa, what is a dildo?' I innocently asked.

'You'll see,' he mysteriously replied. 'But you'll have to wait until another day.'

The following day, the only thing I talked about was a dildo. I absolutely insisted on seeing one. My persistence was such that he finally acceded to my wishes. I was dumbfounded when he produced it, but I demanded that he try it out on me that very evening. I had to admit it was a poor substitute for the real thing.

There was not one variation of pleasure he did not show me and initiate me into. Sometimes he lay on me, his head between my thighs and mine between his knees. With his open, hot mouth, he covered the lips of my cunt and noisily and greedily sucked them. Then he stuck his tongue deep down between them or with the tip tickled my clitoris. In return, I sucked the head of his prick. Squeezing it with my lips, I soon had it all the way in my mouth. I wished I could have swallowed it. At the same time, I caressed his testicles, his belly, his thighs, and his rump.

'Everything is pleasure and delight, when two people love each other as tenderly and passionately as we do,' he was accustomed to say.

Such was the joyous existence I led after the departure of my beloved governess. Eight or nine months rolled by before I knew it. The only clouds on the horizon were the souvenirs of Lucette. I spent happy days and happier nights in the arms of my adored father whom I overwhelmed with my kisses and embraces. How he cherished me! My soul was united to his, and I loved him in a way no words could express.

If the heart remains constant and is filled with the same sentiments, there is always some phantom caprice which pushes us beyond the limit which we should not exceed and carries us much farther than we ourselves desire to go. I was a striking example of that. Do I dare make that confession? Yes. Nothing must remain hidden. I blush at revealing it to my reader.

We have seen the bounty and goodness of my father towards me, the justness of his spirit, and the steadfastness of his character. In other words, he showed how much he merited my love and heart. His image will never be effaced from my heart.

In our house also lived a kindly, devout, aged widow, who spent the greater part of the day in the neighbouring churches. She had three children, the oldest a debauchee in the fullest sense of the word whose companions were of the lowest order. We scarcely ever saw him. He amused himself by squandering the money he had inherited from his father. His younger brother was about sixteen when he left school to join his mother. He was as adorable as a cherub, with a cheerful temperament and a kindly, gentle character.

As for the sister, she was a honey blonde, with pink-tinted cheeks, sparkling eyes, turned-up nose, vermilion smiling mouth, luscious figure, but petite in build, a madcap if you ever saw one, and possessed of an amorous temperament which she cleverly kept concealed. She constantly joked about the sermons her pious mother gave her from time to time.

I became very close to her after Lucette had left, and I made the acquaintance of her younger brother on the few occasions when he accompanied her. Later, there did not pass a day when they did not come to see me and spend the afternoon or evening with me. Their mother was particularly happy at these visits, for she held me up as a model of virtue to her daughter. It is quite true that I had a reserved air that was both inborn and strengthened by my father's example.

I noticed that my father was studying and making up his mind about Vernol and his sister. One day, he told me that Rose knew more than her nanny had ever taught her, and that if she was less instructed than I in sexual matters, which he doubted, she was eager to learn. Also, he mentioned that if I was curious to find out the extent of her knowledge, I was free to do so. The banter Rose and I exchanged afterwards led me to the same opinion as my father, but I could not figure out Vernol.

My talents had been perfected. I was a good musician, playing the harp with taste and singing with feeling, reciting with feeling and consequently, Rose, Vernol and I formed a little society. During our meetings, he made known the depth of his feelings for me. He sought me out on the slightest pretext and followed me ceaselessly. When he was with me, he was in turn attentive, submissive and impertinent, but all his actions told me what he did not dare say. When I became aware of it, I informed my father. My tone was mocking.

'Laura, the first time I saw him, I guessed. When he is with you, his eyes and cheeks become animated. He does his best to hide his embarrassment, but he is not very successful. You can see right through him. Now that you know his love for you, what feelings do you have for him?'

I had never asked myself that question. Up to then, I had considered Vernol merely my friend, and I always addressed him in such a fashion. But my father's query made me think and, on reflection, I had to admit that I was not unsusceptible to Vernol's presence, and that when he was not with his sister, I sorely missed him. When he was absent, I always eagerly asked Rose where he was and what he was doing. It was a mystery to me how a caprice for the likes of him, who was so unlike me, could have taken hold of me. His handsomeness attracted me, to be sure, and his good manners and his winning ways added to his charms.

From my father's look, it was not hard to see that he had discovered in me what I almost did not dare admit to myself. He went for some time without speaking to me about it. I loved him more than ever for his silence, if that were possible. My admiration and affection did not diminish in the slightest, and as a child of truth and simplicity, I was unable to dissimulate. It is claimed that we women are false by character, but I am of the opinion that this so-called sham is acquired and not inborn. Finally, feeling able to sacrifice everything for my loving father, I made up my mind to avoid the pursuit and attentions of the handsome young lad. I was unable to reconcile in my fantasy the feelings I had for Vernol with those I had for my father.

Apparently, my father wanted to put me to the test (for which I was totally unprepared), because one day he took me aside.

'Laura,' he said to me rather sternly. 'I am not very fond of your new friends. Would you please not see Rose and her brother any more?'

I did not hesitate for an instant. Throwing my arms around his neck and pressing him to my bosom, I sobbed:

'If you say so, dear father. Of course, I won't have anything more to do with them. If you wish, you can send them away, or we can go to the country where I won't be able to see them. Let's leave tomorrow. I'll be ready to go.'

Indeed, I started off to pack my things. I was busy at my task when he called me back. Seating me on his knees, he hugged me tightly and affectionately.

'My dear Laurette,' he stammered with emotion in his voice, 'I am overjoyed at your tenderness and affection for me. Your dry eyes tell me that you are willing to make this sacrifice without any pain. Tell me that it is so, I beg of you. Open your heart to me, for there is no doubt that fear is not at the bottom of your resolution. You have never had to be afraid with me.'

'No, father,' I answered simply, 'I have never been afraid of you. I am just following my feelings. I agree that Vernol has given birth within me to an illusion, a caprice, if you wish, which I cannot explain. But my heart is filled with you. When it comes to you, there is not a moment of indecision. I don't want to see him any more.'

'No, my child,' my father quietly declared. 'I just wanted to learn the nature of your sentiments for me, and now I am satisfied. Vernol excites in you sensations that your imagination enhances. You will enjoy them. Also, you will learn the full extent of my tenderness for you, and you will feel that you cannot stop loving me. And that's all I want. Go ahead. I am only jealous of your heart, the possession of which is so precious to me.'

I was stunned. I fell at his knees, my face bathed

in tears and my bosom heaving. I was sobbing so violently that I could barely speak.

'Dearest Papa,' I stuttered, 'I love you and I adore you. In my heart, there is only room for you.'

He was deeply moved at my grief. Raising me up and pressing me to him in turn, he covered my face with kisses.

'Console yourself, my child. Don't you think that I know nature and its immutable laws? Follow your heart, for, as you know, I am not hard-hearted. It is time for you to learn the difference between fatherly love and the love of a lover. I promised you that you will enjoy pleasure with Vernol. As you well know, I keep my word. Besides, he is a nice lad, good-looking and well-mannered. That I have to say for him. If your heart had not gone out to him, it would have turned to someone else, perhaps not as worthy as he. That is the reason for my decision.'

From that day, I felt myself much freer with Vernol. After spending one night in my father's arms, I awoke to hear him telling me between the kisses I was raining on his cheeks that I should pay a call on Rose's mother.

'Tell her to allow her daughter to spend the day in the country with you, and mention, too, that she should not worry if she does not return in the evening for we'll bring her back the next day. As an excuse, we'll say that the coach is being repaired, and you'll keep her here until tomorrow. When you are alone with her, you can find out her inclinations and what she does. She seems to trust you. Once you have wormed your way into her confidence, let me know.'

For a moment, I thought he had designs on her,

but I did not ask any questions. I merely did what I was bidden. For some time, I suspected that Rose was as knowledgeable as I, or almost.

Everything went as my father planned. She came and the door was locked to all comers. All alone, we spent the day in the maddest follies. I played a hundred mischievous tricks on her. She returned them with interest. I bared her budding bosom and made my father kiss the pink-nosed puppies. Her buttocks, her *mons Veneris* and her cunt suffered my playful tortures. I held her in my arms so that my father could repeat my performance, at which she laughed and giggled. Although at times she pretended indignation at some unexpected prank, she lent herself willingly to everything we could think of. Her eyes were glistening and her cheeks flushed.

I partook only sparingly of the collation that was served, but I kept filling her glass to stoke the flames that were already consuming her. After rising from the table, we renewed our frolics. Rose, no longer capable of any resistance, was turned over with her face down on a settee. I raised her skirts, and her bared behind presented a perspective that no painter's brush could reproduce. My father helped me to get revenge for all the tricks she had played on me. I was curious to learn what effect these games would have on her, and when I looked more closely, I found she was almost dripping between her thighs. No doubt about it. She had enjoyed herself immensely during our madcap pranks.

Finally, Rose and I went to my room where we got ready to go to bed. As soon as she saw me in my chemise, she tore it off me. I did the same to her, hurling the last garment to the floor. Dragging me to the bed, she gave me long drawn-out kisses as she fondled my straining breasts and damp matted mount. Immediately, I put my finger on the spot which I guessed would give her the most pleasure. I was not mistaken. She spread her legs and kept cadence with the movement of my finger. Still curious, I inserted my finger into her cunt, and the ease with which it entered left no doubt as to the use she had made of it.

Now I was burning to find out how and when she had lost her maidenhead. I was just about to question her when my father entered the room to kiss us goodnight before retiring. With a sudden jerk, Rose threw off the covers, revealing us completely in the nude with our hands on each other's centres of voluptuousness. She put her arms around his neck, drew his head down, and made him kiss my breasts. Not to be outdone, I forced him to do the same to her seductive gloves. Then I promenaded his hand all over her body, stopping it only at her Venus mount. I could see that he was aroused, but he left us abruptly, wishing us an amusing night.

The clock was striking ten when, the next morning, my father returned to our room and asked, as he awakened us, if we had had a pleasant night.

'We stayed up long after you left, Papa. You saw the mood we were in when you left us.'

Rose, whom our diversions had calmed and sleep had refreshed, blushed and clapped her hand to my mouth. I promptly removed it.

'No, Rose,' I declared, 'you will never prevent me from telling my father everything we did and all you told me. I never conceal anything from him, for I trust him implicitly, as he does me.'

Placing her arms and legs around me, she allowed me to continue.

'When you left us, Papa, Rose was already at a high pitch of excitement. As soon as we were alone, she kissed me passionately on the mouth and began to suck hard on my nipples. She drew me close to her, on top of her. Our legs were interlocked so that our cunts were rubbing one another. My breasts were dangling and grazing hers, and we were belly to belly. Demanding my tongue, she cuddled my buttocks with one hand and with the other tickled my clitoris. By the action of her finger, she invited me to do the same to her. I put my finger on the spot where she was waiting impatiently, and soon we experienced the delights of these amusements. But she refused to let me withdraw it until she had enjoyed ineffable transports four times.'

While I was rendering an account of our gambols, Rose, aroused again by the description and the recollection, had inserted her hand between my thighs and performed what I was telling. I immediately grasped what she was desiring. We had remained in the nude, and I uncovered her. Then I grasped my father's hand which immediately took possession of all her charms. All he was wearing was a dressing-gown which half opened at his movements. From the protuberance straining against the cloth, I could see the effect that the touch of his hands on her body was producing on him. Pointing it out to Rose, I advised her to take off his robe and lay him at our sides. Unhesitatingly, she got up, threw herself at him, stripped him and, enveloping him in her arms, pushed him on the bed.

I was not idle, for I lifted one of her legs on him, and passed the other through his. In this position, his prick naturally was face to face with her cunt, and it goes without saying that I guided the member on its proper route. Her anticipation was so great that she began to quiver like a willow in the wind. With an upward thrust of her derriere, she precipitated the entry into the venereal temple, I fondled her most sensitive parts, an activity she seconded with perfect rhythm. From her passionate transports, we could perceive the excessive pleasure she was undergoing.

My father, who was experiencing the keenness with which she was sucking his prick, was unable to hold himself back. He hurriedly withdrew, and with my hand I finished off the libation that he feared to empty into Rose's cunt. In a delirium, Rose moaned that she had discharged five times while he was in her. Her stomach was inundated with the fuck he was spreading on her. It went all the way up to her breasts. While I was attending to these various duties, she took hold of my cunt which she began to titillate. This little game, together with the emotions caused by the sight of their bliss and the fondlings I was lavishing on them, soon put me in a state of violent agitation.

Now I fervently desired the fire that was devouring me to be quenched. Rose was quick to notice it, and she soon enabled me to join in the merriment.

When we had somewhat recovered from our exertions, I found enough breath to address my father.

'Listen, Papa,' I murmured. You are probably as astounded as I was at Rose's skill, and I won her promise to tell me where and how she had received her training. Now I am going to repeat to you her story, but, no, it is from her mouth that you are going to hear it, and I hope that she is agreeable. What you have just done with her puts her in just the mood to tell you everything without embarrassment and to confide in you all of what she said to me.'

Embraces and kisses were sufficient to overcome her feeble protests.

'Well, all right. Since Laura knows everything already, I have nothing to lose. From what I have gathered, even if I did not impart my story to you, you would get it from Laurette. Moreover, I trust you completely after what we have been through. Yes, it is better that I tell you myself.'

Part Two

THE STORY OF ROSE

'I was sixteen years old when my mother sent me to one of her sisters in the provinces, where I spent six months, mostly in the company of her daughter who was a year my senior. Until that time, I had led a secluded life, always with my mother who is so pious that she never mixes with other people. Since my brothers were away at school, I was either alone or at church with my mother. As you can imagine, I was bored to tears.

'Nevertheless, I liked it better in church than at home, because, although my mother and I sat in the most remote corner in the house of worship, I was aware that someone now and then would have his eyes fixed on me.

'Quite some time before, my mother had promised her sister to send me to her for a stay, since she had often said she would like to have me. I was very eager to go, because I knew that my aunt was the exact opposite of my stuffy mother. It was, however, an unforeseen turn of events that finally caused my mother to keep her word. My oldest brother, who was at home at the time, had contracted the pox, and it was imperative that I leave the house as quickly as possible.

'My aunt and cousin welcomed me with the utmost cordiality. Immediately after a warm exchange of hugs and kisses, Isabelle, for that was my cousin's name, insisted that I share her bed. Although I may have constrained her at the beginning, she embraced me tenderly every night before we went to sleep, and in the morning, when we awoke, I returned her tokens of affection.

'It was not two weeks until we were such warm friends that in the evening in bed, she tucked up our nightgowns to press her buttocks against mine and then give me the four sisters' kiss.

'One night, when I could not fall asleep, although I pretended to, I felt Isabelle's arm make a slight movement. Now her hand was on the upper part of my thigh. Her breathing was heavy and spasmodic, while her derriere gave little twitches. Finally, after a deep sigh, she calmed down and went to sleep.

'Bewildered by her strange behaviour, I at first thought that there might be something wrong with her. The next morning, however, she was her cheerful self, and my anxiety vanished. From that time on, I was aware that she was acting the same way every night. It was a mystery to me, but it was not long before I was to be enlightened.

'My aunt had a chambermaid of about twenty with whom Isabelle was often alone in her room, ostensibly because Justine embroidered beautifully and Isabelle was taking lessons from her. My cousin told me never to disturb her when she was with Justine, for the work required the greatest concentration. At first, I swallowed the story, but when I noticed that she had become as skilful as her teacher, I became suspicious.

'To tell the truth, I was also piqued at being excluded from these tête-à-têtes, and I determined to get to the bottom of the matter. For a young girl, curiosity is the tormenting demon to whom she has to yield lest she succumb herself.

'One day, I found myself all alone in the house, my aunt having gone out with Isabelle, and Justine away doing some errands. Taking advantage of their absence, I went into Isabelle's room to see if I could not find some way whereby I could learn what was going on in there when they were by themselves. After exploring the room, I spied near the foot of my cousin's bed an almost hidden door that I was able to open only after several vigorous jerks. It led into a dim chamber filled with old furniture heaped up almost to the ceiling. The only free space was a narrow passage going to another portal which opened onto a concealed staircase that descended down to a little courtyard from which one emerged into a deserted alley.

'If my aunt thought that she had shut off this part of the house, Isabelle or Justine undoubtedly had discovered the keys. In the furniture-jammed room, I noticed in the wall a bit of drapery that seemed to cover some aperture into my cousin's room. Climbing up on a dusty chair to investigate further, I found a little hole in the cloth through which I could look into the adjoining room. Since it was too small to afford a clear view, I took my scissors and enlarged it so that nothing obstructed my vision. Delighted with my stratagem and determined to take full advantage of it, I beat a quick retreat, closing the door behind me. As I returned to my room, I recalled that when Justine went to Isabelle's room, it was almost always after lunch.

'The opportunity I was waiting for finally came when my aunt went to pay a call on an old friend. Since the matter she wished to discuss was of a delicate nature, she did not take Isabelle or myself. When she was gone, Isabelle made a point of telling me that because she had some new intricate stitch to learn with Justice, I was to feel free to do as I wished as long as she was not disturbed. That was all I needed.

'I made as if I were going for a stroll, but in reality I stealthily made my way to the unlit room, where I hid myself among the discarded pieces of furniture and fastened my eye to the opening. Not long after, I saw my cousin come in with some embroidery in her hand. At the sight of that my heart sank, for I was sure that I was going to spend a boring afternoon and I repented of my curiosity.

'But my hopes rose when Justine appeared and immediately asked where I was. Isabelle replied I had gone to see some friends in the vicinity. Reassured, the maid quickly latched the bedroom door and opened the one of the room in which I was concealed, continuing to the hidden staircase.

'I shook with fright at the thought of being discovered, but she apparently did not notice me as she groped her way down the passage. On her return, Isabelle put aside her work and went to the mirror to arrange her hair. When she began to readjust her scarf and blouse, Justine snatched them off, revealing my cousin's snowy bosom. Taking one of the pink-tipped globes in her hands, she complimented my cousin on their roundness and firmness. Then, baring her own full hemispheres, she compared them to Isabelle's.

'As they were thus amusing themselves, I heard somebody coming up the staircase. Because of the way I was crouched down, I could not see him as he passed by my hiding place. On hearing a scratch at the door, Justine opened the door and then quickly closed it again.

'As soon as the stranger was in the room, I immediately recognized him. He was a tall young fellow slightly related to the family and he paid us an occasional call. His name was Courbelon. Isabelle was not at all embarrassed when he went up and kissed her still uncovered bosom. At the same time, his hand went up under her skirt. When he had finished, he gave Justine the same greeting.

'Taking Isabella up in his arms, he lay her at the foot of the bed where he threw up her skirt to reveal her all. From my vantage point, I could see her flat stomach, her slightly plump thighs, and her rose-lipped slit. She did not have much hair down there, but what there was of it was pitch black. Putting his mouth to the orifice, he tickled its upper part with his finger which soon disappeared in its depths.

'In the meantime, Justine unbuttoned the front of his trousers and brought out an organ of astonishing dimensions which my cousin shamelessly grasped. As he began to replace the finger with it, I heard Justine scold him: "No Courbelon, that I won't allow. If I were to get pregnant, I would know what to do to avoid unpleasant consequences, but if Isabelle ever got into that condition, where could the two of us hide ourselves? Caress and fondle her as much as you like, but just don't you dare put that into her."

'That discourse, which I heard distinctly, was a complete enigma for me. I saw Courbelon reluctantly withdraw the member and grumblingly titillate Isabelle, who was clutching his masculinity as she had before.

'A short time after he had resumed the game with his fingers, I heard and saw the same sighs and motions that she made when we two were in bed together.

'Now I had a glimmering of what had been happening. She had been doing to herself what Courbelon was now doing to her. Now that it was over, Isabelle rose from the bed, and Justine, who had been watching them like a hawk, threw herself in turn on the couch. With one arm she embraced the small of Courbelon's back, and with the other she gripped the truncheon as she dragged him down on her. In a twinkling of the eye, her skirt was up to her navel. Resting on her stomach, he massaged the pearl-shaped breasts which he then covered with feverish kisses. Judging from the convulsive movements of her flanks and derriere, I gathered he was inserting his member into her. I would have given anything to see it go in.

'From behind, my cousin passed her hand between his bucking buttocks, either to fondle his testicles or to measure how deep the member had penetrated.

Now both were seized by spasms. They must have been in seventh heaven. It seemed that Courbelon was dying after a violent explosion. When he pulled out his instrument, it was no longer its proud self, but a humble, self-effacing creature diminished in length and thickness. I thought it rather resembled an earthworm. Exhausted, they paused for several moments on the bed, after which the kisses and embraces were resumed.

'This opening scene, which thoroughly delighted me, was soon followed by a second act which aroused my emotions even more.

'Impatient with their hampering garments and aware that my aunt would not be back until dusk, Courbelon tore off their clothing, and in an instant they both were as naked as the day they were born. In proportion, Justine's figure was not the equal of Isabelle's, but her skin was whiter and more satiny and her body more rounded and contoured. Playing no favourites, his lips alternated rapidly between the bodies of his two enticing partners. And their bottoms, breasts and slits were his to do with as he wished.

'What I regarded avidly for more than half an hour lit fires within me and excited emotions I had never before experienced. The caresses of the intertwined trio became more animated. Now Courbelon made his two lovely partners lie on their backs, side by side, then on their bellies, with their legs spread wide apart. I saw as clearly as Courbelon all that met his eyes. He examined them carefully, kissed their slightly arched buttocks, and stuck a finger of each hand between their thighs. In the meantime, his instrument was restored to its pristine condition.

'Because Justine could not see him from the position she was in, Courbelon took advantage of the situation to introduce the monstrosity into Isabelle. Suddenly, however, Justine became mistrustful and abruptly sat up. When she saw what he was doing, she grabbed the miscreant by the neck, nearly choking him, and dragged him off of his willing victim.

'I was furious, for I was following the course of the implement with the deepest interest, and Justine had to ruin it all.

' "No, no," she stated firmly. That is not permitted. I've told you the reason a hundred times, and you're just going to have to give up the idea."

'Since I could hear as clearly as I could see, I did not miss a single word or phrase.

' "Come now, my dear boy!" Justine said in a conciliatory tone as she took hold of the offender. "Why don't you just put your prick into my cunt? They are old friends, and you don't run any risk with me!"

'She was too late, though. Before inserting it in her, she gave it two or three shakes. At that, I saw Courbelon lean on her shoulder, holding one of her breasts and kissing it, as he spilled out a white liquid I had never seen before. The spurts were accompanied by a series of convulsions that marked the depth of his rapture. For some unknown reason, the sight nearly drove me out of my mind.

'Without realizing it, I had been irritating the upper part of my slit in the same fashion I had seen Courbelon do to Justine and Isabelle. I was engaged in this stimulating occupation which gave me nothing but unalloyed pleasure. Suddenly, Justine and my cousin, undoubtedly animated by the caresses he had lavished on them, put him in the same state they themselves were in, namely, complete stark nudity. From head to toe, there was not a stitch of clothing on his body.

'This new perspective attracted my eyes to him with a delicious curiosity, for unknowingly, that is just the way I had wanted to see him. As I regarded them, it seemed that their enjoyments were all that I had ever desired. Justine and Isabelle were caressing him, kissing him, fondling the now lifeless virility, and cuddling his testicles and buttocks. In return, he kissed them, massaged and sucked their nipples, turned them over on their backs, looked minutely at their rear cheeks, and excited them by inserting and withdrawing his fingers in and out of their apertures.

'As this went on, I noticed his instrument slowly regaining all its former pride. The organ, with which he playfully menaced the laughing girls, looked like a pike about to be stuck into the body of a ferocious beast. There was no mistaking Courbelon's desire for my cousin, but Justine, taking a firm hold on him, forced him with her back down on top of the bed. For a moment, I thought he was going to split open 'her stomach, but she was not to be daunted.

' "Let's wait a moment," he suggested to her, "so that we may enjoy our raptures simultaneously."

'Placing Isabelle on the bed, he spread open her knees and thighs between which Justine put her legs, also spread apart. Since there was nothing to hinder my view, I was able to see Courbelon's truncheon sink into her aperture, only to reappear, vanish again, and so on.

'It seemed inconceivable that such a fearsome object could ever enter my opening, which was so tight I could barely get my little finger into it. And I never dared push it too far because of the sheer agony it caused. But Justine's example lent me courage, and I determined not to worry about the consequences, no matter what they would be.

'While Courbelon had his prick in Justine's cunt, his finger was ensconced in Isabelle's. He turned my cousin's head by telling her that she possessed the most charming Venus mount he had ever beheld. After saying the same about her slit, he recommended her to stimulate her clitoris, a suggestion she promptly followed as he slipped his finger in and out in regular cadence with his thrusts into Justine.

'Steadfast in my determination to follow their example, at least in part, I took a deep breath and plunged in the forefinger of my left hand as deep as I could, all the while stirring it around in imitation of the movement of Courbelon's prick. Gradually, a delicious sensation invaded my whole being, and I now realized why my cousin took such a pleasure in a repetition of the game.

'It was not long before the trio was wallowing in utter ecstasy. Isabelle, still on her back, was wiggling her backside like a shimmy-dancer from the South Seas. Witnessing her transports, Courbelon suddenly shouted in glee: "Darling, you're coming!"

'Scarcely had he finished uttering these words than he fell almost senseless on Justine's bountiful bosom after sighing deeply and mouthing oaths to describe his bliss. Justine, after agitatedly twitching her rump, also remained prostrate.

'These evidences of impassioned enjoyments roused me to such a pitch of excitement that I, too, sank back exhausted against a piece of furniture, undergoing at the same time an ineffable gratification. What an excess of delight to feel for the first time such a hitherto unknown voluptuousness, a delight never dreamed of. Such bliss lifts one out of this world and, for too brief a period, it is the only thing that really exists.

'During the subsequent period when I was savouring to the full my complete contentment, the three performers in the adjoining room were starting to put back on their clothes. As soon as they were decent, Courbelon tenderly embraced the two girls and made his way out as he had come in. A few moments later, Justine and Isabelle also left the room. As for myself, I waited a while longer to emerge from my place of concealment and, taking the same route as Courbelon, I regained the inhabited part of the house. Shortly afterwards, my aunt returned in company with Isabelle, who had gone out to meet her.

'From that time on, I thought and dreamed of nothing but what I had witnessed. Their words were still ringing in my ears and their actions were still before my eyes. Not for a moment were my reflections far from that living tableau.

'That very evening when I was in bed with Isabelle, I pretended that I was sound asleep and Isabelle fell in a profound slumber. Since it was apparent that she was not going to do anything to me, I had to seek resources within myself, and I followed her example. But the following evening was an entirely different affair.

'As soon as we were in bed and my cousin thought I was asleep, I became aware that she was starting her little game again. Knowing now full well what was going on, I turned over and, placing my thigh on hers, I put my hand where I knew she had her finger. I slid it under and immediately had her whole mound in my palm. As I fondled her tenderly, I kissed her budding breasts and inserted my finger into her slit. Then I withdrew it to tickle the spot where I had found hers. When she spread her legs and let me have my way with her, I heard her abruptly heave a deep sigh and, to my amazement, I found her all wet in the area where my hand was.

'Now overcome with the urge for the same to be done to me, I gripped her hand and covered my own hillock with it. Forcing her digital extremity to do its duty, I soon found myself returning sigh for sigh.

'She was not a little surprised at all I was doing, for she believed me as innocent as the day I was born. Knowing that I had been raised in a strait-laced puritanical home, she had been wary about imparting to me any of her secrets for fear I would blab everything to my aunt or mother.

' "Well, Rose, how is it that you are so experienced?" she asked curiously. "I am really amazed."

' "That I can believe, my dear cousin, and I'll tell you on the condition that you won't be angry with me and that you will keep on loving me," I replied.

'The moment I said it, I regretted having opened my mouth and was reluctant to continue until Isabelle, taking me in her arms, tenderly pressed me to go on and tell her all.

' "You aren't afraid of me, are you?" she asked. "I

assure you that you can count on my discretion, and I solemnly promise never to say a word, particularly not to our mothers."

'Reassured, I recounted all I had witnessed and how I was able to be a witness. When I had finished, she was aghast at what I had learned.

' "Oh, Rose, my dear Rose, I beg you never to reveal my secret. If you betray me, I'm lost."

'I vowed to be as silent as the grave, and my cousin said she was not even going to tell Justine that I knew After I had calmed her fears, she rained kisses on my face and body, all the while questioning me closely on what I had seen and heard and the impression it had made on me. I gave her a full account, including my own reaction. Now that she knew of my own misdeeds, her last lingering doubts vanished. Now it was my turn to satisfy my own curiosity.

' "But tell me, Isabelle, how did you happen to fall in with Justine and Courbelon?"

' "I'll do so gladly, cousin," she replied. "Since you know everything, there is little point in holding anything back, and besides, I am sure that you will not break your promise.

' "About four or five weeks before you came here, I had gone out with my mother to pay some calls, but having forgotten my bag in my room, I went back alone to get it. After I found it, I went to Justine's room for some reason or another. Since the door was partially open, I entered without knocking.

' "What met my eyes nearly stunned me. I was stupefied to find Courbelon on top of her in the strangest position. When he noticed me, he quickly got off his mount, but not before I saw his organ which he hurriedly tried to conceal at the same time he was lowering Justine's skirts that were up to her navel. Although she was dismayed at being discovered, she was relieved that it was not my mother who had found out her guilty secret. I began to leave right away, but Justine, fearing that I would tell what I had seen, ran after me, got on her knees, and begged me with tears in her eyes not to reveal her shameful disgrace. Her pleas were so heart-rending that I promised all that she wanted and kept my word.

' "I'll admit to you, dear Rose, that the incident gave rise to many thoughts and conjectures which kept running through my head. From that time on, Justine often came to my room under the pretext of giving me embroidery lessons, but, in reality, the instruction was of a completely different sort. She taught me things I had never dreamed of. She bared my bosom and played with my breasts as she depicted in the most vivid colours the delights of sensual pleasure. I have to admit that I was all ears.

' "Finally, one day, her descriptions so aroused my curiosity and latent sensuousness that my cheeks were flaming, my breath was coming in short gasps, and my bosom was rising and falling. The eager questions I threw at her enabled her to sense that the moment she had been waiting for had come. She took me in her arms, lifted me up, and bore me to the bed, where she raised my skirts. Vaguely sensing that she wished to play forbidden games, I feebly tried to stop her, but she was undeterred, telling me that any handsome young cavalier would be overjoyed to be in her place and regard and touch the beauties she was gradually exposing. His organ would swell and then he would expire rapturously, giving me at the same time the most unimaginable delights. Her flattery, lascivious descriptions and caresses had completely reduced my defences, and I let her do with me as her fancy dictated.

' "Then she placed the tip of the finger of her left hand between the lips of my opening which she titillated, while with the right she rubbed my clitoris."

' "My dear cousin," I interrupted her, "why don't you call a spade a spade and use the terms I heard Justine and Courbelon employ?"

' "You're right, Rose," she conceded. "I should have remembered that I don't have to be careful about my language with you.

' "After some moments of this treatment, I finally experienced that supreme sensation she had described in such glowing terms, even though she told me that the pleasure would be tenfold greater with a gallant young man. Ever since then, we have often been playing this delightful game, much to my satisfaction. One day, she went so far as to stick her finger in me. I felt some pain at first, but it soon went away. It was not long before she was teaching me how to return the favours she was bestowing on me, which I did, and not simply out of a sense of gratitude.

' "A week or so before your arrival, my mother went to make some calls without me, enabling Justine and me to resume our joyful diversions, but this time we were completely in the nude. I did not know it, but Courbelon was hidden behind a curtain witnessing all our merry pranks. As I was to learn later, it had been planned between him and Justine.

' "As he emerged from his place of concealment,

also in the nude, Justine nearly burst her sides laughing to see him in such a state, but I nearly fainted when my eyes caught his enormous erect sceptre. I wanted to flee, but my feet refused to move. Besides, bare as I was, I could hardly leave the room. Trembling and filled with shame and fright, I tried to take refuge behind the curtain, but as I made for it, the two of them stopped me in my tracks. After what Courbelon had seen Justine and I doing, I could scarcely put up an effective resistance.

' "Courbelon held me tightly in his arms, passionately kissed me, and ran his hands and lips all over my quivery body. Finally, my shame gave place to desire. He put the baton in my hand, but it was so thick that my fingers could not encompass it. The fire of his kisses and caresses and the sight of Justine fondling his muscular body set me ablaze, and I was in no state to refuse him anything he wanted. The joys into which he plunged me were so profound that I almost lost consciousness. Justine acted as his able assistant.

' "But the two of them did not stop there. Dragging me to the bed and holding me down with one hand, she made me look at Courbelon's prick which was losing itself in her cunt. From the vivacious expressions on their faces, I had a fair guess of the bliss they were undergoing.

' "Yesterday was the sixth time they allowed me to have the pleasure of their company. You can imagine that we would have had more gatherings had it not been for the fear of discovery. When I learned of your forthcoming visit I was overjoyed, for I hoped your being here would give me more freedom. I confess I was mad to have Courbelon do to me what he always did to Justine, even though Justine had repeatedly warned me of the dangers of pregnancy and I was still awed by the proportions of the desired object.

' "But on closer reflection, I noticed that it caused her no pain. The suffering must be less than the pleasure. Consequently, I decided that my fears were groundless, particularly when Courbelon reassured me on that point. Justine was adamant, but it was hard for me to believe what she said when she was always doing exactly that which she prohibited me."

'When she paused for breath, I urged Isabelle to gratify me as she had been. At first she refused, but I used every argument my innocent mind could come up with. I know that they were not very convincing, but I did not let up. Whether from curiosity, fantasy or coincidence of desire, I do not know, but she finally yielded. From that time, we enjoyed almost nightly what we called our "secret", and we became inseparable.

'A little later, we were invited to a wedding in the village, the bride being a relative of Justine who would be sure to attend. Isabelle laughingly mentioned that it would be a good opportunity to put one over on her Cerberus, for I had been continually urging her to find a way to realize her ambitions with Courbelon. Now was her chance, I told her, and she should not let it go by. I added that my aunt, believing we would be at the celebration together, would take advantage of our absence to visit with friends. All Isabelle had to do was stay in her room, while I went to the wedding, where I surely would find Courbelon. As soon as I saw him, I would tell him that Isabelle was waiting for him to discuss an important matter and that he should go to her room.

'At first, she shook her head and said blushingly that she could not do such a thing. But I kept after her, and with my caresses which stimulated her desires, I prevailed in the end.

'My aunt had already left when I walked to the village. The first person I saw among the merry throng in the banquet room was Courbelon, to whom I gave unnoticed the message from Isabelle. As soon as I had finished, he was gone in a flash. Momentarily, I regretted not being at my observation post, but I consoled myself with the thought that Isabelle would render me a detailed account of all that took place and abandoned myself to the pleasures of the ball.

'When Justine spotted me alone, she immediately inquired why Isabelle was not with me. I replied that I thought she was with her mother for a while, but that she would surely return soon to take part in the festivities. Justine swallowed the story hook, line and sinker, but as time went by and there was no sign of Courbelon, she became suspicious. It was obvious that Courbelon's absence and Isabelle's tardiness were causing her to smell a rat.

'When she seemed at the end of her patience, Courbelon made his appearance, followed by Isabelle a few minutes later. At the sight of them, Justine immediately vanished. I guessed that she had surmised Isabelle had just come from the house. When she came back, there was nothing to be read on her face, but, as we later learned, she had made some inquiries, the answers to which gave her all the information she needed.

'Isabelle turned down all invitations to dance, and when she whispered in my ear the reason, I loudly declared that I, too, was tired from the exertions and was ready to go home. After asking our farewells, we walked back together to my aunt's house. You can imagine my impatience at hearing what had happened, and it seemed an eternity until we were in bed.

'When I tried to put my hand on the spot which should have undergone the assault, she pushed it rudely away, saying that it hurt too much to be touched. There was a moment of silence before the whole story poured forth like water rushing over a dam.

' "Ah, my dear Rose, my curiosity has been satisfied,' she said in a woeful tone. 'Courbelon came promptly to my room when I was eagerly awaiting him. As soon as he opened the door, I flung my arms around his neck and wet his face with my kisses. In turn, he fondled and explored every corner and recess of my body, without my putting up the slightest semblance of resistance. After these preliminaries, he inserted his hard baton in my hole that he had lubricated with his saliva, but you have no idea of what torture it was. That monstrous member was tearing me apart. Not daring to scream, I burst into tears.

' "He tried his best to comfort me by assuring me that the next time I would experience nothing but pure unadulterated bliss, but he deceived me again the second time. His following attack resulted in nothing but redoubled anguish for me. I suffered the unbearable. When he presented himself the third time, I refused him outright, but he was so insistent

with his kisses and embraces that I had to yield to
his entreaties. He was as gentle and tender as he could
be, but it did not help. I could not stand the torment
any longer. The stabbing pains along with the fear of
getting big with child so terrified me that I shoved
him from me with such violence that he did not dare
try again. Right now, it feels as if there is fire burning
between my thighs. That is why, as I told you, I just
could not dance."

' "My darling cousin," I told her consolingly,
"since you are younger that Justine, it is quite natural
that yours is much tighter and narrower than hers."

' "That's what Courbelon told me. He said that
with time and practice my slit would get wider, but
in the meantime I am suffering the agonies of hell."

'When she had finished, it was late, and we were so
tired that we fell into a deep sleep almost immediately.

'The next day Justine called Isabelle into her room
where she simply told her that Courbelon had been
in my cousin's room the night before and that the
door to the hidden staircase was not locked as it
should have been. Moreover, on the rug she had found
some petals of the boutonniere he had been wearing.
If that were not enough, she found the bed rumpled
as if two people had romped on it. Finally, she had
learned that Isabelle had not been with her mother,
as I had said, but had remained in her room before
she left the house more than two hours after I had.

'Although she realized Justine knew what had gone
on, she refused to admit it. But the evidence was so
damning and Justine was so persistent that she finally
made a clean breast of it.

'Either fearing what the consequences might be to

Isabelle or angry at Courbelon for his behaviour, Justine put so many obstacles in their way that they scarcely had a chance to speak to each other, let alone to be by themselves. There was no doubt that Justine was also jealous. Whatever the case may have been, she employed every means at her disposal to break up the affair and watched over their every movement.

'Because of these blockades placed on the road of true love by Justine, Courbelon finally became irritated with his mistress, with whom he soon had a falling out. When he had to move to a remote province, he quickly forgot her as well as Isabelle. Shortly thereafter, Justine left both my aunt's service and the village. Isabelle suspected that she had given up her post to rejoin Courbelon, for whose sake she would have made any sacrifice.

'At first, Isabelle was almost inconsolable at losing him. Whenever we were alone, she always turned the conversation to him. Although I was getting sick and tired of hearing the same old thing day in and day out, I comforted her the best I could and in the end, I succeeded. The pleasures we shared enabled her to bear her loss with more fortitude, and finally she had dismissed him completely from her mind. I have to admit that I was sorry at losing him, for I had entertained high hopes of participating sooner or later in their gambols. But her ever-growing affection for me soon effaced his memory.

'All together, we spent four delightful months in each other's company. During this time, she instructed me in everything she had learned from her former teachers and soon we were able to add a few embellishments of our own.

'Thinking back on this period of my life and the answers Isabelle gave me to the many questions I plied her with made me realize that Courbelon probably had had designs on Isablle from the very day she discovered him with Justine. It seems likely he had persuaded Justine that the best way to guarantee Isabelle's silence was to admit her into their games, and she fell into the trap. If it had not been for her jealousy and mistrust, he most likely would have gained his ends.

'The time that I spent at my aunt's sped by all too quickly. I knew it had to come sooner or later, but I almost burst into tears when my mother wrote saying that she wanted me back with her. My departure was a lachrymose one on all sides. My aunt was so touched that she promised to do everything she could to have me return. Since Isabelle and my aunt knew how to enjoy life, their hearts went out to me, because they envisaged my spending bleak, dreary days with my devout mother who had no social life whatsoever. That was what I thought, also, but the way things turned out proved us all wrong.

'Once back with my mother, I turned to account everything chance and Isabelle had taught me. Like her, I was able to procure for myself the most delicious pleasures every day. More often than not, I allowed myself a double measure. My stimulated imagination was concentrated on one thing, and on one thing only: a man. Every time I came near one, I could not keep my eyes from him. It mattered not if he were young or old – I wanted him to quench the flames that were consuming my entire being.

'Just about that time, my brother Vernol came

home for his vacation. The first thing I noticed was how handsome he had become. That surprised me for apparently his charms had escaped me before. It is true that we always had a good brother and sister relationship, but now I found that my feelings for him had changed completely. In him were united all my yearnings, embers that unknowingly he was stoking. I had eyes only for him.

'For a long time I itched to have him touch and fondle that which I had only let Courbelon glimpse, but I was humble enough to believe that I was too young to be able to attract the attentions of an older man. Besides. I was positive that his male organ had grown in size during his absence, and the thought of Isabelle's trial momentarily frightened me. But that cloud on the horizon quickly passed: and I determined that I was going to have Vernol.

'His room was behind my mother's where I also slept, and when that devout woman departed for church where she spent two or three hours every morning, I quickly locked the door after her. The servants, believing that we were still sleeping, never bothered us. That was my opportunity to go to his room while I was still in my nightgown and tease and annoy him in a thousand ways while he was still in bed. I kissed and tickled him. Other times I would yank off the blankets and sheets so that he was almost naked and then playfully spank his backside which was as soft and tender as a girl's.

'When he had enough, he would leap out of bed and start chasing me. Usually, I let him catch me, whereupon he threw me back on his bed where he paid me back in full for the slaps I had given him.

'We had given ourselves up to these games for two mornings when, on the third, the sport took a different turn. That time, when he hurled me on the bed, my nightgown flew up to my waist (with a little help from me). He looked at me and then at my little cunt. He seemed stunned. Recovering himself after a few moments, he first feasted his eyes on my thighs, gingerly touching them with his hands, and then spread them apart. I made no protest.

' "Ah, Rose," he exclaimed. "This is the first time I have noticed what a difference there is between us."

' "What do you mean, difference?" I innocently replied, feigning ignorance.

' "Take a look for yourself," he cried excitedly as if he had just made a great discovery. With that, he pulled down his trousers and showed me his little implement that I had only half seen before. Under my gaze, it grew in length and rigidity.

'Taking the lance in my hand, I stared at it carefully, tenderly stroked it, pulled the foreskin back and gently rubbed the tip.

' "Let me look at you some more," Vernol begged, impatient to do the same to me.

'More than willing to grant his request, I lay back again on the bed. Raising and spreading my legs, he scrutinized my private parts with the attention of a scientist peering into a microscope, but it was obvious that he had not the faintest idea of their functions. Now he was on his knees, bent over me. Running my hand between his thighs, I grasped the pretty pigmy and amused myself by taking off and putting back on the hat covering the coral head.

'The pleasure I perceived I was giving him

augmented mine, and I was all agog. Straightening up, I reversed him on his back as I completely bared the toy to my view. I kissed it, I nibbled it, and I caressed its little olives. Finally, by means of rubbing my hand up and down on the erect baton, I succeeded in releasing that white fluid I had seen Justine's hand produce with Courbelon. I could not get over the delightful sight of the jets making an arc in the air. He looked as if he did not believe what was happening. In his regard astonishment was mingled with bliss. His hand on my thighs became crisp and then remained motionless.

'Reclining on the pillows, I put my arms around him and made him do a little thing he was totally ignorant of but which I was dying to have. He obliged, and I was soon in that state of ecstasy in which I had put him.

'I was delighted at how extraordinary he found all that was happening, for I had led him from surprise to surprise. I resumed my sweet attack on his innocence by fondling again his instrument, which I then began to kiss and suck. I had it all the way in my mouth. If I could have swallowed it, I would have cheerfully done so. Now he was back again in that state which every normal woman dreams of.

'Up to then I had not dared to teach him how to put it where I most wanted it, but I became bolder and more shameless and snatched off his nightshirt as I pulled mine over my head. Now there was nothing to prevent me from contemplating his charms in their entirety. I covered them with my hot hands and lips, while he gratefully returned the favour. When his boyish prick was as hard as it ever was going to be,

I made him get on top of me and guided the member to its proper home.

'What an apt pupil he was! Although I was tight, he was not big. Energetically, we shoved ourselves against each other. Now straddling him, I finally succeeded in getting all of it into me with the ineffable satisfaction of realizing that I was going to get what I had so passionately desired for so long. With shudders that ran through both of us, we simultaneously and reciprocally rid ourselves of our not exactly intact virginities.

'Dear heaven! What sensuality we enjoyed! Vernol was almost out of his senses with ecstasy. We experienced that unadulterated felicity which comes only once in a lifetime and which cannot be described in mere words. Our bliss was at its peak. He was the first to savour that glorious excess when he discharged. As he gushed into me, his arms which had held me as if in a vice suddenly became limp.

'Quickening my tempo, I reached the goal instants after, and as I collapsed like a punctured balloon, he knew that I was in the same state of wonderment as he. Glued to each other, we tasted to the dregs that magnificent annihilation which is no less exhilarating than the transports that caused it. Being the first to recover from our swoons, I found that I had immediate need of his hand and finger again.

'Every morning we indulged in this most delightful of all diversions, either in his bed or mine, and during the rest of the day, anyplace where we felt ourselves secure from prying eyes. At night, when we could not be together, I resurrected by myself the day's pleasures while he did the same in his chamber. I knew that because he told me himself. Every morning we exchanged confidences during the realization of our nocturnal illusions.

'Impressed from the very first by all that I had taught him, he urged me to tell him where and how I had acquired my knowledge. At first deeming it imprudent to say anything about my stay with my cousin, I skirted the question with vague generalities, but as our intimacy deepened and my confidence in him grew, I told him the whole story.'

When Rose finished her tale, which she had told me before in more vivid detail, especially about Vernol, I took the floor.

'Dear father, you don't know what else Rose confided in me. She didn't tell you everything.

' "My dearest Laura," she said to me, "Vernol is head over heels in love with you. I saw it right away, and he even admitted it to me. Now, I am not jealous at all, for I love both of you tenderly. You are lovely and he is charming, and nothing would give me greater pleasure than to see you in his arms. Yes, my dear, I would even put you there myself, for his happiness means all the world to me." Don't you think she is slightly out of her mind, Papa?'

'Not very,' my father replied after some thought. 'As a matter of fact, I really am not surprised at all.'

It was easy to see that Rose adored pleasure with a fury. When we told her that, she readily agreed. The tableaux that she had summoned up from the past animated her as they did us. The effect on my father produced an eloquence which Rose immediately seized upon. To show us the delight she found in the beloved object, she slid it into her sanctuary with a prolonged sigh.

After she had reached her climax seconds before my father, she resumed her reflections.

'If you feel that you cannot confide in me after what I have told you about my brother, please disabuse yourselves of the notion. Because of our intimacies since yesterday, I feel free to tell you everything that is in my mind and heart.'

'Come, Papa, and sit next to your daughter,' I interrupted. 'I'll take Rose's place and prove to you that I am every bit her equal. But put that thing in her so that she can experience at the same time the joys you have given me.'

'Well, Rose, you are going to play a new role,' he declared as he rose to fetch the dildo, which he then fastened to her waist.

Rose was ecstatic at the intrument, the likes of which she had never seen before. Making me mount her, Papa guided it into my cunt while telling her to bestir herself like a man and titillate me at the same time. Also, he instructed her how to discharge it when she felt that I was on the verge. Then he got on me in turn and introduced my old playmate into the rear aperture.

As Rose wiggled most lasciviously, she held my breasts as I fondled hers, and when she sucked my tongue, I thought I was dying. Just as I was about to lose consciousness, she released the dildo's contents. My cunt was inundated. At the same time, the fuck that my father spurted into my rear lifted me to new raptures. Rose was not left out of the general bliss, for the rubbing of the dildo against her clitoris had produced an orgasm. I finally succumbed completely, slain by sheer bliss.

My father soon came to, and when I was revived, we all three got out of bed since it was almost noon.

When we were back on our feet and in our clothes, Rose could hardly wait to examine more closely the marvellous strange contraption. After explaining that it was an exact replica, if slightly oversize, of the male organ, I pointed out its features, chiefly the mechanism which jetted hot water or milk so cleverly that the recipient could not distinguish it from real semen.

When I was through, Rose promptly tucked up her skirt and tried to introduce it into her cunt. Her awkward attempts were so comical that I could not help but laugh. My peals were so loud that my father came back into the room to learn what was up. When he saw Rose fumbling with the instrument, he shared my amusement.

'Leave it alone, Rose, because it is not functioning for the time being,' he advised her. 'Besides, we have better things to do.'

When she desisted and began rearranging her dress, he took me by the hand and led me out of the room.

'Laura,' he earnestly began, 'Rose will be the victim of her own passion and fiery temperament. There is no holding her back. Already she is abandoning herself to pleasure with a fury that I have never before seen in a woman. You can bet your last franc that she will pay a heavy penalty for her excesses. The same goes for that poor Vernol whom she has started down the same path. But I wish to take advantage of it in order to carry out some plans that I have in my head.'

Leaving me, he went to find her in my room. Naturally, I put my ear to the door.

'Rose, what you said about your brother's feelings for my Laura is evidence of the deep friendship you two girls have for each other. But can we count on Vernol's discretion as we can on yours? It is absolutely necessary to be sure of this, as you can well imagine.'

'I don't think you need have any worry on that score,' she assured him. 'What could he gain by blabbing except expulsion from our society, which would be unthinkable in view of his sentiments for your daughter. I'll vouch for Vernol, and I beseech you to let him join in our fun. If he were prevented from pouring out his heart to Laura, he would die of grief.'

'All right,' my father consented. 'It seems that everybody is in league against me. For the time being, however, I don't want him to have the slightest inkling of our activities, and I demand your promise that you will not breathe a word. If he knew, he would consider me well compensated, but I insist on his paying me himself for the sacrifice I am making for him. Just forewarn him that he can expect anything and that he will have to consent to anything we demand of him.'

'I'll answer for him as I would for myself,' Rose warmly replied, 'and you can be sure that he won't learn a thing from me without your consent.'

'One thing more,' my father continued. 'I want both of you to know that Laura is my daughter in name only. She is not my flesh and blood, but she is no less dear to me for all of that. Nobody but you and your brother must know of this.' My father's voice was stern as he gave that warning. 'Now, go to your

100

mother with Laura and tell her that we are going to spend the day in the country tomorrow. With her permission, we would like to take you and your brother with us. And promise me that you and Laura will behave yourselves until the time when we can give free reign to our fantasies.'

When the colloquy, of which I did not miss a word, was over, Rose came to get me. We hurried to her mother who readily granted my father's request. Leaving my friend to her own resources, I spent the rest of the day with a cousin who lived nearby. In the meantime, my father was supervising the arrangements for the next day's project.

At night, when I was nestled in his arms, I asssumed he was going to tell me about his talk with Rose and the excursion the following day, but he fell asleep without saying a word. Disappointed and frustrated, I soon followed his example.

Early the next afternoon, there stopped before our gate a coach which carried us to a charming villa at some distance from the city. Since I had never seen it before, I suspected that it belonged to one of his friends who had placed it at his disposal. Vernol had done his best to improve on his native attractions, and Rose and I were wearing fetching summer dresses in the latest style. Since Rose had explained certain matters to him, he was more at ease and self-assured. When we finally arrived about four, the weather was still perfect.

We made several turns in the gardens whose natural beauty was not crushed by the artificiality so in style today. From among the shrubbery and the flower beds, we gazed at the horizon whose iridescence seemed to be in accord with our mood. After the promenade, we entered the house and went through the suites of rooms. In the main salon where my father led us a delicious repast was being readied for us. As we consumed the appetizing dishes, my father was not sparing with the superb wines he poured.

Whether it was the juice of the grape or some other stimulant, I do not know, but we soon felt its effects. Our heads were whirling as we pelted each other with the petals from the flowers of our garlands. When father noticed the state we were in, he dismissed all the servants with orders not to return until they were summoned. Now we were by ourselves.

We were almost staggering as he led us to an apartment which we had missed on our tour, for it was situated in the most remote part of the villa. From there he ushered us into an intimate salon illuminated on all sides by candles in holders at a height at which they could be easily extinguished by hand. Below them and all around the room ran mirrors with drapes hung in festoons. Scattered around the chamber were big easy-chairs, very low and almost without backs, which were covered with large soft cushions.

On the walls hung various paintings, but what paintings they were! Heavens! In his wildest flights of fancy, Aretino himself could not have conjured up such images. Also, there were statues of figures in highly suggestive positions. In an elaborately decorated niche was to be seen a piece of furniture which sensuousness and voluptuousness had converted into their throne. The surroundings and the wine now dispelled the last of our inhibitions. We were seized by a sort of delirium, with Bacchus and Madness leading the frenzied dance.

Rose, inspired by her favourite deity, Venus, gave the pitch and commenced the hymn of pleasure by flinging herself at my father's neck, embracing Vernol, and hotly kissing me with an invitation to follow her example. Snatching the scarf that covered my bosom, she threw it to her brother and then sailed hers to my father. She made the men kiss her rosepointed globes and then transferred their lips to my welcoming hemispheres.

These frolics reflected infinitely in the mirrors around us aroused us to dizzying heights of lubricity. Our cheeks were flushed, our lips parched and burning, our eyes glittering, and our hearts pounding madly. Vernol, whose clothes were already in disarray, appeared to me as beautiful as the dawn with his glowing complexion and dancing eyes. I regarded him with the adoration of a god, all of whose attractions were concentrated into a single object in the centre of his body, it being the object of all my desires. Although he was unaware of what condition it was in, my father perceived its gradual growth.

In trying to force me down on one of the settees, Rose called for her brother to help her. By parting and lifting my robe, she enabled him to see that for which he was pining. I tried to get revenge by reversing her on her back in turn, but she beat me to it. She threw herself down on it, and kicking her legs up in the air, she unashamedly displayed all the gifts nature had endowed her with – her fetching cunt, her rounded bottom, her flat belly and her satiny thighs – all were visible to the eye.

Immediately, the three of us were at her side to lavish on her the caresses she made clear she so ardently desired. Scarcely had we placed our hands on her buttocks than, with two or three spasms and a roll of the eyes, the fountain of pleasure gushed. Rose and I soon perceived that my father and Vernol had erections straining at their bonds. With an abrupt movement, Rose was at my father's side.

'Dear Papa, I threw you my scarf. That means you will be my husband, and I shall be your wife. Give me your hand!' she imperiously commanded.

'Willingly, my dear Rose,' my father answered, 'but the ceremony only takes place at the end.'

'That is all right with me,' she assented. 'But Vernol caught Laurette's. We have to bring them together, don't you think?'

'Just as you wish.'

She hurriedly took our hands which she clasped in each other's. When she made us kiss, our mouths obediently obeyed the order. Placing her hand on my bare bosom, she pronounced us man and wife. If our senses were overheated, Rose was on fire.

'How refreshing it would be to have a bath. Right now,' she exclaimed. 'I feel as if I were burning up.'

My father rose to pull a cord in the alcove. When he did so, the throne slid back, revealing a pool with three taps that sprayed cool, warm, or hot water.

'Isn't this marvellous?' Rose chortled gleefully. 'It's an enchanted palace. I'm going to be a naiad, but not all by myself.'

In a flash, she appeared wearing the usual costume of water fairies, namely, nothing at all. Grabbing hold of me, she urged my father and Vernol to aid her in stripping me to a similar state. Before I could utter a word, I was down to the buff. When Rose made a signal, Vernol pranced out like a satyr. That left only my father, whom Rose and I were busily disgarbing.

My furtive eyes were already scrutinizing Vernol. What a handsome and seductive figure he cut! He bloomed with the freshness of youth, and in the middle of all the alabaster whiteness of his skin, skin that a young girl would have envied, proudly rose the distinguishing mark of a man.

Consumed by devouring flames, we were like those furnaces which sizzle when water is thrown on them and then only burn hotter. Two pointed lances were aimed at Rose and myself, but the prospect of combat did not daunt us. Our bodies prey to the frisky hands and lascivious lips of the Tritons, Rose and I happily returned their advances instead of rebuffing them and toyed with their arrows as they manipulated our quivers. At that moment, my father was prudent enough to shove a sponge into mine when I was least expecting it.

Vernol wanted to enter the lists against me, but with the adroitness so natural to women and so calculated to stimulate desire, I nimbly stepped aside and sprang out of the tub. When Rose followed me, the men were soon out, too. The effect that the dip had on them was visible from the condition of their crests. Their temporary humiliation gave us a chance to dry ourselves and don diaphanous robes which concealed nothing from their larcenous eyes. Then we all stretched out languorously on the easy-chairs. Hardly had we settled ourselves than my father, giving a jerk on another cord, had lowered before us a table heaped with delicacies and wines like those that had intoxicated us shortly before. All was there to augment the ardour which was rising again in us.

Vernol was so impatient that he was twitching as he reclined on his chair. What surprised me was Rose's seemingly unabated exuberance. As for myself, for whom voluptuousness was a more refined enjoyment, I preferred to wait and watch before attaining the goal. The anticipation gave me almost as great pleasure as the realization. My father was also firmly of the opinion that the postponement of satisfaction gave it more spice when it was finally tasted.

Consequently, Vernol and Rose had to chafe under the yoke of unrequited desire. It was easier for Rose who, under our touches and fondling, had reached bliss three times already, according to her own admission. She called the collation a wedding banquet, even though no maidenhead presided over it. But what did it matter? Voluptuousness held sway, and we were content under her rule. Crowned by the sylvan deity, she was to be seen in the centre of the table with the sceptre in her hand. In the four corners of the alcove were entwined pairs in the most lascivious positions. Flitting among them were old envious satyrs making their pitiful offerings which the nymphs scornfully refused, for here all was merriment and animation.

The impetuous Rose, with a bottle and a glass in her hand and robe open to reveal her seductive conniceties, sent flames racing through our veins. What she poured us became a torrent of fire. Now I was boiling inside, and our partners were in the same state of lust, judging from their virilities.

No longer able to restrain herself, Rose lifted her

glass and cried out: 'Vernol, take your bride?' Then, throwing herself into my father's arm, she again shouted: 'And here I have my husband!'

She had firm possession of his prick, which she was getting ready to insert into its proper slot, and Vernol had one arm around my waist and the hand of the other on my cunt, when my father put a stop to the proceedings.

'Just a moment, children!' he announced. 'There is a condition I am laying down for my consent to continue, and it is only right that it be met. If Vernol is to penetrate Laura, I insist on following the example of that courtier who, after coupling his wife with a young page she was sleeping with, did in the lad's rear what the latter was doing in the lady's front. Therefore, if Vernol wants to fuck Laura, I demand that his bottom be at my disposition.'

So, I thought, Vernol's charms had attracted my father as much they had me. At first, I felt a twinge of jealousy, but then I reflected that I would be freer with Vernol if my father was not watching me, and I did my best to enhance the pleasure of their game.

Roughly ripping off Vernol's robe, I made my father an offering of his rump, the rounded cheeks of which I spread wide. Oblivious to my actions, the boy was preparing to plunge his prick into my chasm.

'No, no, Vernol,' I chided him as I would a naughty child. 'Don't deceive yourself into thinking that you can put it into me without fulfilling that stipulation my father made.'

'Oh, Laura!' he panted. 'You can put any obstacle in my path and I shall overcome it. I have been in hell for an eternity, and there isn't anything I wouldn't do to have you and expire in your arms.'

'We can't leave Rose out of our little party,' my father said, interrupting Vernol's impassioned declaration.

The table was whisked away, and a thick soft mat covered the flooring over the pool. Now the alcove was a true sanctuary of lust. In a flash, we relieved ourselves of all that we had not entered the world with. Adorned only with what nature had seen fit to give us, we made obeisances at the altar to the divinity we all worshipped from the bottom of our hearts.

On all sides the mirrors reflected endlessly our various charms. When Vernol cast admiring glances on mine, he swept me into his arms and covered me with kisses and caresses, while his prick, which I was firmly clutching, stood as firm as a rock. My father was massaging his buttocks with one hand, while with the other, he was busy with Rose's breasts or slit. She, in turn, was all over us.

Finally yielding to his amorous frenzy, Vernol turned me on my back, widened the space between my thighs, kissed my Venus mount and valley, darted his tongue into it, sucked my clitoris, mounted me, and finally jabbed his prick into me up to the hilt.

In the meantime, my father had taken his position behind him. Rose, on her knees and supporting herself on her elbows, and with her fur-fringed cavern before my face, spread still wider her brother's rear cheeks, noistened the entry with her tongue, and guided my father's prick along the path she had cleared. While they were bucking up and down in rhythm, she impartially was tickling the testicles of each. In her cunt I had my finger, which I energetically kept pushing in and out. Again, it was she who first came to bliss, but Vernol was not far behind. When my father noticed his victim's sudden stiffening and relaxation, he redoubled his efforts which added greatly to my pleasures. Keeping time with his quickened tempo, I plunged down the dizzy descent of ecstasy along with him, and we landed at the bottom side by side. The three of us were now, one could say, a single unit which Rose was bathing with her wet lips

When it was over, we paused to catch our breath. Still breathing heavily, Vernol asserted that he had never experienced such raptures in his life.

'What you have received you should give,' my father drily remarked. 'Come, Laura, let's see what he can do. Although he is not so well equipped as I, I am quite sure that you will not be dissatisfied with him. While he and I taste of your delights. Rose will repeat her performance, but this time she will stimulate your clitoris with her hand from behind.'

Jumping on my sire, I feverishly caressed his body as Rose introduced his prick into my cunt. After this task was performed, she parted the cheeks of my derriere and took her brother's virility into her mouth. When the organ was sufficiently hardened and moistened, she led it to its goal. She titillated me as she massaged her brother's buttocks. At the same time, my father, his finger in her slit, was nearly driving her out of her mind with lust.

When the sublime presence was announcing himself, we all flew after it and caught it. Oh, how magnificent and superb he was! We all spurted, drenching ourselves with the fluid that began dribbling down the sides of our bodies. I was in such a rapture that I could barely contain myself. After floundering around like a drowning swimmer, I felt come over me a calm, that was no less voluptuous than the climax itself. The contraction of my muscles and the friction of all the sensitive, delicate parts where sensuousness reigns were almost too much.

There was no question but that we had to get some rest. We were able to persuade our male partners to put back on their robes, if only for the time being, but that did little to soothe our taut nerves. Our eyes, hands, mouths, and tongues all bespoke desire, and our conversation concerned nothing else. Rose's and my breasts, buttocks and cunts were massaged and reverently kissed, tokens of affection which we returned on their pricks, nipples and testicles. There was no mistaking the reaction – the vanquished members had risen proudly to renew the struggle with our distended clitorises.

Now Rose had a role with more meat than those she had played before. After I had made her lie down with her knees raised, my father rested himself along side of her, and passing his thighs under her legs, he aimed his prick at the target.

Joining the fray, I got on top of her with her head between my knees and those of Vernol, who was doing it to me in the fashion of a dog. I put my father's instrument into her slippery slit where it went in and out like a piston. In turn, he played first with my breasts and then with her opulent pendants. As he was thus engaged, Rose and I amused ourselves by irritating each other's rosy buttons. She could not keep her fascinated eyes off Vernol's prick which was

rising and falling in time with the swaying appendages. It produced such a powerful effect on her that
during the time we were striving for the initial ecstasy,
she had savoured in four times. Four times she
moaned in a dying voice, 'I'm coming! I'm dying!'
She was an inexhaustible fountain. A fifth copious
overflow blended with my father's boiling jet, one that
flooded her.

With their pleasure prodding us, Vernol and I
reached the summit almost simultaneously. This time,
Rose seemed as if she were parting this life. The bliss
she had been chasing had not escaped her eager grasp.
Her cunt was a morass of fuck and no wonder, for
she had three or four orgasms to our one. After
writhing and biting and scratching, she fell into that
prostration in which one feels nothing but the most
delicious fatigue.

When she came to, she could not praise highly
enough the variation and she made up her mind that
she could study it more closely. As soon as we came
to, we changed places. I took her place, with her on
top of me, while she was being fucked by her brother.
Since my head was between their thighs, I was able
to follow at close range all their motions. At the same
time, my father gave free rein to his fancy with me.

When this fourth act was over, we were so broken
that it was imperative to take time out again. After
we unsteadily got to our feet, my father had the table
lowered again and we gulped down the food as if we
were famished. Sleep was also a necessity. As soon as
the table was lifted away, the four of us lay down on
the matting, one on top or beside the other, our arms

and legs interlaced, and each clutching the object of his desires.

After an hour of respose, Rose, awakened by a sultry dream, shook us out of our lethargy. Our gambols commenced anew, but instead of rushing headlong into the maelstrom of sensuousness, we toyed with our urges in order to make them last longer and enhance their intensity. We made advances to pleasure and then pushed it away but, aroused in turn, it pursued us. Only Rose allowed herself to be captured, and she surrendered two or three times before it abandoned her to catch up with us. We were just as helpless before its might. It is not a thing to be trifled with. We finally ended the day with a fifth act, in which Rose played the leading role.

As she was lying on my father who was taking the main highway on her body, Vernol presented himself at the rear gate. I assumed her former position, rendering them the same services I had received. At the same time, my father had his wandering hands all over the hills and dales of my body. Perhaps for the sake of change, Vernol from time to time took different roads. He veered from the one I had started him on to join up with my father on his path. Rose was overjoyed to see them united in such a way, side by side on the same narrow way which barely accommodated the two of them, but at the last moment, he returned to the thoroughfare I had chosen for him. She found this, too, utterly divine. It was not difficult to please Rose.

'Death would be sweet if it came at such a delicious moment!' she cried enthusiastically.

Although we smiled at her flight of fancy, we found

it quite in keeping with her temperament and mentality.

Before dressing, my father made the pool appear again. Without any ado, I immersed myself in its refreshing water. The others promptly followed me. I pulled out the sponge and vigorously washed the hole it had occupied. This second ablution calmed our nerves, and since it was getting late, we made preparations for our departure. The coach appeared at eight, and we were back in the city an hour or so later.

During the ensuing days, Rose kept after me to play similar games with her. I finally yielded, and I have to admit I enjoyed them. But after a while, the sport palled, a fact which my father noted with his sharp eyes. He was not displeased. And I began losing interest in Vernol. My initial infatuation with him merely resulted from the impression made on my eyes and hands. I felt nothing in my heart for him. If you took away his good looks and manners, there was not much left. Finally, it was over and I had few or no regrets.

From then on, I followed only the dictates of my heart which led me back to my father, whom I loved and adored more than ever. I considered him an extraordinary man, unique, and a true philosopher far above the mundane, but at the same time appealing and seductive to a woman's sensitivities. He had the qualities that hold our fair sex in fetters and that can clip the wings of our inborn inconstancy. Thinking men make no protest when they are faced with it, but they are able to put a stop to it. Finally,

I was in reality the sole object of his affection, just as he became to me. These feelings for him, and several incidents, caused me to break off completely my tenuous liaisons.

An adventure during which Rose snapped several lances with too much insolence caused my final alienation from her and Vernol. Added to that was the account of a particularly loathsome adventure they confided to me. Now I was convinced that fastidiousness was not to be found in either of them and that their emotions were ruled only by unbridled lust and passion. Their way of life and thought was not in accord with mine at all.

Since I rarely saw them, they took their pleasures where they found them, and their favourite hunting ground was the public park. One day, as Vernol was taking a stroll on the promenade with his sister, he came across four of his old school comrades, the oldest of whom was about twenty. Joyfully, they recognized each other, embraced, and hurled questions and answers back and forth.

'Where are you coming from? What are you doing? Where are you going? Who is this bewitching creature?'

Rose, of course, did not take their flattery and compliments amiss. Once their curiosities were satisfied, they insisted that Vernol and his sister join their party and go with them to an inn where they had planned a light meal.

At the outset, the young people obeyed social conventions, but the oldest, who was also the craftiest, began to exert his wiles for his underhanded purposes. As they briskly paced to their destination, the polite language turned into double-entendres and off-colour jokes and stories.

Once in their room, Rose flounced on the bed saying that she was hot. As she did so, she revealed her snowy bosom and a well-turned leg. Such praise was rained on her charms that she nearly reeled with delight. After the meal had been consumed and while the wine was being drunk, heads became giddy. Rose tossed off some more champagne with the others following her example. In the general hilarity, the innuendos became more unmistakable and liberties were freely taken and given. Touches became embraces and embraces led to kisses. The fire was lit and soon was to blaze.

The senior, more brazen and experienced than his companions, took Vernol aside and told him what they had planned. At first, he looked stupefied, but then he held his sides with laughter. Curious as usual, Rose insisted on learning what the joke was about. After succumbing to her wiles and pestering, he told her that before they had met her and Vernol, they had agreed among themselves that the one of the quartet with the biggest prick would pay for the wine and the one with the smallest would pay for the rest.

When she heard that, Rose almost choked with merriment. She was so convulsed with laughter that when she fell back on the bed with her legs up in the air she revealed practically everything that a woman should keep concealed.

'Who's going to be judge?' she demanded when she had recovered from her hysteria.

'Why you, of course,' the senior replied as if it were the most natural thing in the world.

Animated by the wine and flattered by the invitation, Rose declared that she was well qualified to take on the judicial chore.

From that moment, all restraint was cast aside and the inhabitants of the room were shameless in their antics. A valiant and battle-scarred warrior, Rose held her own with the best of them and was prepared and ready for more interesting assaults than verbal ones. Eager to bring matters to a head as quickly as possible, she beckoned Vernol to her, and wrapping an arm around his neck, she forced his head down to kiss the breasts she had flipped out of her bodice. Then sliding her other hand down to his trousers, she undid the buttons and yanked out his straining prick.

In revenge, he slipped his hand up under her skirts where he quickly won possession of her cunt that was already beginning to dribble. When she kicked up a knee, her centre of pleasure was visible in all its glory to the others. The sight so awed the group that they eagerly gathered around her. One took hold of a posterior cheek, another a part of the thigh, still another one of her snowy globes. Each now had a part of her. As she made Vernol rise, she asked if any of them could produce its equal. At that, each immediately had a competitor in his hand. Now before her eyes was the dazzling spectacle of five proudly standing pricks, arrogant and menacing, which dared her to combat, even though they knew they were sure to lose.

Sitting up for a better view of the jousting site, she gave the quintet's pride and joy a quick but careful scrutiny.

'I could come to a decision right now,' Rose

asserted, 'but as a judge, I want to take every possible precaution. I'll have to use some sort of measure, even my own if necessary, so I won't be accused of making a biased judgment. Let's begin.'

Using her boot-lace as a tape, she conscientiously took the measurements of each, both in length and diameter, and with the same care weighed their appendages in her hand. Manipulating all these instruments of pleasure affected her so deeply that she fell on her back again. The two or three convulsive wiggles of her derriere were evidence that she was discharging.

It was as if they had heared the starting signals of a race, the way they rushed to mount her.

'Before we proceed,' she said, stopping them by imperiously raising her hand, 'I wish to announce my findings. I hereby order the senior to foot the bill for the wine. If my brother had been a party to your pact, he would have been obligated for the remainder of the bill, but since he wasn't, I bestow that honour on number two.'

Seeing the latter's crestfallen expression, she comforted him by saying that it would grow with his years and that he would be the first to have her, which would be very soon, since all those pricks and testicles had set her aflame.

Stretching herself flat on her back, she beckoned to the lad, who needed no second invitation. He leaped on her and in a flash, his dart was in the ring she proffered him. Vernol followed him in turn, and then came the three others according to the gradations she had measured. The overjoyed Rose was wallowing in fuck and bliss. Spurting almost incessantly, she scarcely had time to catch her breath, for no sooner had one left the lists than another took his place.

There finally came the moment when she could not any more, and the entr'acte was spent in drinking, laughing and cuddling. She was willing prey to the impassioned kisses and foraging hands of her five gallants. Since they did not tolerate a stitch of clothing on her, she was promptly in the state of the goddesses during the Judgment of Paris.

The ravishing sight revived their forces and desires to a fury. Wistfully, she wished she had five cunts so she could have enjoyed them all simultaneously, but she had to be satisfied with having them in twos.

Always impatient for variety, she made the champion lie on the bed with his head at the foot, and then climbed onto him so that her breasts dangled directly above his mouth. The least favoured youngster got on her between her thighs. When they were in position, they each took the indicated road. Now squeezed in a tight vice, she clutched the envious members of the other two, while she took Vernol's bauble between her lips, alternatively sucking and tickling it with her tongue.

Although sperm was running down all over her body, she remained unconquered after twenty-five engagements during which time she irrigated the field of battle twenty-nine times. She was worn out, but deliciously so.

I saw her the following day. At first, I thought she was on the point of death with her languid eyes and listless body. Surprised at finding her in such a sad state, I questioned her and kept at it until she and Vernol told me all about the orgy.

I did not bother to give them any advice, for I knew how useless it would be. I did not even deign to scold them. The reader is undoubtedly aware that they resumed their former activities as promptly as they could. That was the last time I saw them, but I heard about their ends.

Unable to stop herself in her mad drive for pleasure. Rose finally succumbed to it. When she stopped menstruating, she had an abortion, which took a terrible toll on her. She suffered from agonizing fits of dizziness and her sight began to fail. She more resembled a walking wraith than a human being. The cheerful spirited young woman had vanished. Finally, the lingering illness brought her to the grave.

Vernol, who was his sister's faithful companion in all her escapades, shortly after came down with a virulent fever which nearly carried him off, and no sooner had he recovered than he contracted the pox which permanently disfigured his handsome features. It was not long before he was laid to rest at Rose's side.

My father had foreseen that something like this would happen, and afterwards, we often discussed it. Better than ever, I knew the good care he had given me, and my gratitude knew no bounds at having escaped such a tragic fate. Our relationship gradually deepened, but the feelings we had for each other were more tender, more sensuous and refined than passionate. Many nights we spent together in bed with no sensation other than the quiet satisfaction of knowing that the other was there.

One evening, I suddenly remembered all my past indiscretions, which I now considered acts of infidelity, and I burst into tears. Immediately he was at my side, comforting me and asking what was wrong.

'How can you have any esteem for me after the way I treated you?' I sobbed. 'I'm nothing but a debauchee who was unfaithful to you.'

'Have you taken leave of your senses, my child!' he asked in astonishment. 'What does it matter if a woman has lain in the arms of another lover, if her heart and mind remain true? Is the worth of a woman to be judged by how often she has been used? And wasn't I then unfaithful to you with my dalliances with Lucette, Rose, and even Vernol? And yet you know that there is nobody whom I love as much as I do you. So no more much nonsense.'

I was reassured and comforted.

Then tragedy struck. Its first heartless blow had been the death of dear Lucette, the news of which saddened us, my father even more than myself. Although he was his usual kind self always, I noticed a change in him afterwards. Many times I caught a sombre expression on his face.

I was twenty when my father, the most lovable man who ever walked the face of the earth, for whom I would have cheerfully laid down my life, caught pneumonia, and all the arts of medicine were unable to save him. Day and night I was by his bed which I wet with my tears as he feebly ran his hand through my hair. The end came and his last sigh was breathed on my lips.

What a loss! I was more devoted to him than if he had really been my father. He had introduced me to the Count de Norval, to whose amorous activities I owed the light of the day, and whom I regarded with no emotion other than a slight curiosity.

My grief was such that I nearly went out of my mind. I could not even find surcease in sleep since it never came. Soon I, too, came down with a fever which turned into a serious illness. I wanted to die, but my hour had not yet come, for my youth saved me against my will.

When I regained my health, I determined to bury myself alive. Having lost everything that counted, I loathed life. I entered a convent.

If it had not been for the solicitude of Eugenie, I am sure I would have perished behind those forbidding walls. Without knowing the cause of my sorrow, she was still able to touch the bottom of my heart. Never was she too busy to come and dry my tears and dissipate my apathy. Her tenderness and sympathy lent weight to her consolatory words, but the night toppled all that she had built during the day. That she quickly recognized, and she obtained permission to share my bed. I was surprised at the treasures concealed beneath her wimple and robe. When she found that my spirits had picked up some, she urged me to tell her the whole mournful story.

After her kindness, I could not rebuff her and I began recounting my life piecemeal. I knew that I needed a friend, but I despaired over finding one again. It was at such moments that I realized what I had lost in Lucette. And I never dreamed that I would find a replacement in Eugenie. As our intimacy deepened, I repaid her confidences with mine, and in her arms I found the balm for my pain.

Never shall I forget a certain night when she spoke to me even more tenderly than was her wont.

'Dearest Laura,' she said, squeezing me to her, 'I know that you're suffering, but if I can dull the edge of your grief by confiding in you what I am undergoing and have undergone, nothing would make me happier. Listen, my dear, I love you. I love you with all my heart, even though a cruel fate has decreed that I have to wear a religious habit.

'Hypocritical nuns surrounded my innocent childhood with walls and bars and sucked me into their infernal dungeons. Ignorance and prejudice are my tormentors and desire my executioner. During the night, I am unable to shut my eyes because of the tears that fill them. By day, I am disgusted or bored with all I see and hear. Compare yourself to me. At least, you can leave here whenever you wish to give a lover the charms that I have glimpsed and am now touching.'

The soft hand that she placed on my breast sent a thrill running up and down my spine.

'He has come back to me!' I cried deliriously. 'I lost him to death, but now he has been returned to me.'

As I tightly pressed her to me, it was my father whom I was embracing. Such was the illusion she had produced in me. But as I ran my hand over her body, there was one thing lacking that snapped me back to reality. But her other delicacies that I tasted with my tongue compensated for the lack. Her bosom, her figure, her derriere, her skin and her mound were incomparable.

'What a delight it would be for you if only a lover

could hold you in his arms as I am now,' I ecstatically exclaimed. 'You once said you wanted to know about these forbidden pleasures, and if the raptures were as great as they were claimed to be. Now I shall give you some idea, that is, if you wish.'

Her curiosity and desire, both at white heat, led her to accept my invitation. For my part, the wish to console her and tear away the veil of ignorance made me forget temporarily my own woes. She proved to be an apt and conscientious pupil.

Spreading apart her legs, I grazed with my fingers the lips of her narrow cunt whose roses were just starting to bloom. I did not dare insert a digit, for the initial pain would hardly be a suitable introduction to enjoyment. Soon, however, I won the throne of voluptuousness with its fetching clitoris that I slightly irritated. She was thrown into a spasm of ecstasy from which she had the greatest difficulty in recovering.

'Dearest Laura,' she murmured weakly, 'I never dreamt that there was anything like this in the world.'

She in turn awkwardly made me her lover and my body was covered with impassioned kisses and feverish hands as she tried to return the raptures I had given her. But I was still too sad at heart to be receptive, and I stopped her hand. Instead, I took her back in my arms and, renewing my tokens of affection, I put her on the first step towards bliss.

'This is so wonderful,' she sighed. 'Do anything you wish to me, but never stop.'

When my hand slipped back to her darling little cunt and I started to probe it, she squirmed at the exquisite pain.

'It is I, dear friend,' I whispered into her ear, 'it is

I, happiest of mortals, who plucked your maidenhead, that rarest and most sought after of blossoms.'

Now that she had taken the first sip of sensuousness, I no longer hesitated to open my heart to her completely and I recounted to her all the adventures set down on these pages. If I was able to free her from the yoke of ignorance, it was no problem to rid her of the last vestiges of prejudice. After telling her of my own experiences, the fear of pregnancy no longer troubled her.

'Everything you tell me and do to me runs counter to what the nuns have taught,' she panted.

Her trust in me, my counsel, and my assistance brushed away the last crumbling obstacles on the road of sensuality. The peace of mind she enjoys today was due entirely to my efforts, and her lover owes his victory to me. Yes, my friendship served them both well.

Before completing her education, I wanted to meet the Monsieur Valsay so dear to her heart, make sure of his character, and ascertain if he was worthy of her love, her confidence and her favours.

When I met Valsay, I liked what I saw and heard. I felt no qualms about letting him have Eugenie, rouse and satisfy her yearnings, enlighten her and banish her fears.

Yet, had it not been for me, Eugenie would never have completely overcome her timidity. When he pressed her with the most heartbreaking importunities to make him happy, and she refused him, even though she desperately wanted him, I took his side. At the mment when her ardour was becoming almost too much for her I decided it was time for me to intervene, only too happy with the thought that I was contributing to their felicity.

Now I am going to remove the last of the hindrances,' I informed them. 'Valsay, you will be a pure ingrate, one unworthy of the inestimable prize I am about to bestow on you, if my conduct toward this end lowers me in your esteem.'

Earnestly, he assured me that that would never happen.

In spite of Eugenie's protests, I closed the door of the reception room and then almost dragged her to the grille against which Valsay was pressing his face. I did not forget to tear off her veil. There he eagerly grasped for her saucy breasts, kissed her lips, and sucked the tip of the tongue she stuck out in spite of herself.

His overpowering desire gave him courage to insert his hand up inside her skirt to reach and possess the *mons Veneris*. I pushed her still closer to him, kissing her for reassurance at the same time. Finally, he was able to raise the robe up to her waist and contemplate that delightful little cunt with all its ornaments of untouched youth.

His hands wandering over her yielding body were like tinder on her inner bonfire. Vainly he cursed and kicked the implacable grille that separated us and opposed his desire. My heart was almost breaking at the touching sight.

'What?' I taunted him scornfully, although I did not mean it. 'Are you so lacking in resourcefulness that these bars are going to be an insuperable barrier to what you say you so ardently want? True love always finds a way. But I also love Eugenie, and I shall prove it, for there is nothing more I want than to make the two of you happy.'

The squares formed by the iron bars were larger further up. First, I firmly tucked up the hem of the black religious garb which contrasted so dazzlingly with the alabaster of her firmly rounded rump, which he massaged, kissed, and paid the homage due to it. Then I got down on all fours and made her stand on my back so that the little slit was framed like a picture by the bars of the upper square. Valsay, unable to withhold a gasp of admiration, pulled up a chair on which he stood to be at the same level as she. Almost yanking out the organ in which all his desire was concentrated, he thrust it into her hollow as I slipped my hand through her thighs to assist him. Slowly but surely, that sensation we term passion began to exert its irresistible pressure on her. She was swaying back and forth on my back, when I felt her stiffen. A few hot drops of liquid dropped down on my skin.

Just before he was to emulate her, he discreetly withdrew and spattered my back like a hailstorm. Then I left the happy couple to their own devices.

When Eugenie saw the jewel I had so often described and praised, she took it almost gingerly in her hand and fondled it, but it was apparent that she still did not know quite what to do with it. Bashful about admitting her ignorance, she made muffled laments which quickly brought me back to her side, and when I was there, she beseeched me not to leave her. Generously, I offered to lend whatever further assistance was required. Now she was as gleeful as a child with a new toy.

It was then that I reminded her of the beneficial

sponge, about which I had told her. When she returned with the primitive contraceptive, I had a chair ready for her to supplant my back. Touched by my thoughtfulness, she insisted that I stay to witness the consummation.

With her hand, she exposed to me the divinity between Valsay's legs. Then she revealed to him my breasts, which, to my surprise, I found had retained all their curvaceous charm, and everything else that a decent woman keeps concealed. She even permitted him to touch them. If they only knew what a jerk of emotion they aroused in me.

When I whispered to her how I felt, the little traitoress shamelessly blurted out my secret to him. She was insistent that I, too, enjoy the favours of her lover. She wanted me also to have the most precious thing she owned. When she tried to make me take her place on the chair, I resisted in spite of her pleas and urgings. The blood in my veins had turned to lava, but I still held fast.

'No, Eugenie,' I said firmly. 'I shall never consent to something like that, no matter what you say. After all I suffered, I made up my mind to renounce any intimate relationships with men, and I shall not be shaken from this resolution. In spite of the sensations you have awakened in me. I am happy and content just to lie and rest in your arms at night when you quench the flames that you lit during the day.'

With that, I hurried away to let her lose her virginity without me.

A fate jealous of my contentment decided to destroy it. Eugenie and I were separated when urgent matters concerning my inheritance forced me to leave the convent sooner than I had intended.

As I had promised, I wrote her almost daily during my absence. Even through letters, we remained as close as we ever had been. She knew the attraction she held for me just as I knew how she cherished me.

As I conclude this account, I sigh for the warmth of her arms around me and her lips on mine. Inwardly, I send her a thousand kisses which I hope soon to be able to give her personally. When we meet, I shall have for her a little jewel similar to Valsay's but not so dangerous, but one which will fill a certain gap. Since Valsay has been recalled to his regiment and will be gone for some time, the perilous liaison will fade away and I shall soon be at her side to dry her tears.

Wait for me, my dearest.

My Conversion
or The Libertine of
Quality

Preface

Monsieur Satan:

During my adolescence, you were my instructor. It is from you that I learned all the tricks that served me so well during my early years. I have followed your dictates faithfully, as you know, and in return, I have exerted myself night and day to expand your empire and increase the number of your subjects.

But, Monsieur Satan, things have changed. You must be getting old, for you stay down in hell. Even the monks are unable to persuade you to come out. Your younger devils, poor fellows, don't have as much knowledge as our apprentice pimps. The reports they bring you are false because the women cheat and fool them.

I am discharging now my debt to you by dedicating this book to you. In it you will learn what is going on in the court and the doings of women, financiers and devouts. You will read about some escapades in which you would have been delighted to participate.

May the tableaux I am about to present to you revive your sense of ribaldry, and I hope that everyone who reads this work will have an erection.

My most respectful regards,
Your Diabolic Highness,

CON-DESIROS [Cunt Lover]

Up to now, my friend, I have been a bad lot. I have pursued beautiful women, and I have been hard to please. But now that virtue has returned to my heart, I see the error of my ways. From now on, I am going to fuck only for money. I shall be a stud to middle-aged women and instruct them in amatory games at so much a month.

Already I think I see a clod of a woman on the verge of finishing her forties offering me the flabby thickness of her ample body. Fortunately, there are patches of pristine freshness still to be found on her dumpiness. Her ruddy sagging tits are in agreement with her piggish eyes in expressing something other than modesty. She rubs my palm, for the financieress, like her senile husband, rubs everything to make it move. I have the decency to blush.

Ah, somehow that pleases me. My eyes sparkle. My virginity is stifling me, for you will recall that I still have that precious jewel which I am most anxious to rid myself of. I am given much more than I expected. With alacrity I start to show my gratitude.

Damn it! I can't get an erection. It is because of the woes that overwhelm me. My creditors are snapping at my heels. . . .

When my hand wanders, she becomes animated. How gentle I am, but, at the same time, cunning! The tempo becomes a spirited throb. My voice is an *adagio* with a lively *presto sostenuto*. Ah, take a look at how milady's bottom is bouncing up and down. Her bosom is heaving, her windpipe wheezes, her cunt dribbles, she is beside herself and she wants to carry me along with her in her rapturous wave.

Oh, please, take it easy. I am in such pain. She

132

makes me an offer, but how can I accept money from a woman whom I esteem so highly? When she doubles the ante, I weep. The gold appears. Gold!!!! ... A miracle! No sooner do I spot it than I get a hard-on and fuck her.

After this easy victory, I pay my respects to Madame Honesta, the last of her line. Her home is redolent of rectitude and respectability. Everything bespeaks abstinence including her face, the features of which are not exactly such as to inspire tender sentiments. Her cheeks are pinched and her figure slightly on the scrawny side. In all honesty, I am unable to praise her bust, although a gauze scarf permits me a glimpse of what there is of it. One could have wished for a better turned leg, although it does taper into a dainty foot.

Her talk concerns her nerves and headaches and a husband she never sees except at meals. Are you going to say that a woman like her would never pay anything? Don't be fooled. Of course she will, because she is vain and prides herself on her generosity.

At first we observe the conventions by exchanging witticisms and gossip and making epigrams and *bons mots*. Madam is right when she comments that it is a very agreeable morning.

A bonnet is delivered. Dear God! It must have been designed by the Graces themselves. The deity of style fixed the blossoms to it, and all the zephyrs are playing in the plumes that cover it. How this plum colour perfectly matches the English green! But who is it from?

You can easily guess that I am the guilty one. The culprit blushes. I pout and sulk as I betray myself.

Victoire, Madame's maid whom I have won over with a few kisses and coins, pleads my cause during my absence.

'Ah, Madame, if you only could hear how he raves about you. He's such a kind gentleman and far better than that chevalier who is always at your heels. I know that he would never cause you a day's grief. His man told me that he doesn't toy with women's hearts like so many men nowadays.'

'But do you think that I am. . . ?' Madam stutters.

'What an utterly stunning bonnet! It becomes you perfectly. Why, you don't look a day over twenty when you have it on.'

'Don't be a little fool. Don't you know that I am thirty, and even a little more?'

('More' indeed. That has been common knowledge for over ten years now.)

In the afternoon, I return and find her alone. I apologize for my intrusion. Freely granting me pardon, she becomes tender and I passionate. Then we . . . . (Damn it! The woman is in such a hurry that I am in danger of losing what I paid out for the hat.) But I was smart enough to have told my flunky to come and remind me that I have an appointment with the Minister. With an audible sigh of regret, I kiss the hand that trembles in mine and take my leave.

While this is going on, I strike up an acquaintance-ship with one of those women who, jaded with life, seeks pleasure at any cost. She approaches me because, with her honour, her reputation, her high moral standard. . . . Bosh! Those have all gone the way of her youth. The bargain is quickly struck. She pays me and I am in her. But I refuse to discharge, and she knows it. She pesters the life out of me.

Ah, beloved money! I sense your august presence. I am stubborn and we languish in a stalemate for two solid weeks. Finally, I modestly give her to understand that while I hold her in the deepest affection, I have certain obligations. . . . Is that all that's the matter? . . . She gives me a princely sum. . . . My gratitude knows no bounds. I rush into the arms of my benevolent Messalina and experience, not exactly pleasure, but the satisfaction of knowing that I am not an ingrate.

Tired of her? What do you expect? When you have crammed the hen, it doesn't lay any more eggs. The fees become less frequent, and I frequently fall asleep. – *What? You go to sleep?* – Yes, during the night, and what is more, in the morning, too. The beloved morning which gives life to hope and throws its light on amorous combats. When she complains, I get angry. She sputters about misbehaviour and ingratitude, but I show her that she is wrong, for I leave her.

Plutus, come and inspire me! A god does appear in answer to my prayer, but he does not have the happy attributes. It is the deity of good sense, the busy-bee Mercury. After consoling me, he sends me to Monsier Doucet. I am sure that you don't know this gentlemen, so listen.

A figure that seems taller because of a long cassock and cloak, a face beginning to show the ravages of time, a ruddy plumpness, the eyes of a lynx and a jaunty wig. His open honest visage on which wit has left its imprint beams with complacency. The only time he smiles is when he wishes to reveal two rows of perfect white teeth. Such is the most fashionable confessor in Paris. Throngs of the female devout wait in his reception room and the consultations never cease.

His favourites are those spinsters and widows entombed in a perfect quietism of conscience but whose hinges swing all the more easily because of that. The man of God conceals under his sanctimonious demeanour an ardent soul and several admirable talents. You correctly surmise that it is my intention to reach these women.

I worm my way into the good man's confidence by letting him know that I am almost as much of a hypocrite as he. He puts me to the test, which I pass with flying colours, and introduces me to Madam ****.

Her home is a mausoleum of saintliness. The luxury is solid and unostentatious. But – a young man like me with a lady of impeccable reputation and virtue? Right you are. My visits become more frequent and our familiarity increases.

One day, as we are leaving church where she had dragged me to hear a sermon, I start making comments on the other women who were present. Note how garrulous she becomes.

'What did you think of Madame Y****.'

'Good heavens! Her feet are like barges.'

'But she is pretty.'

'She could be if she knew how to apply cosmetics. But she would never have any fresh complexion.'

(You can imagine how her colour heightens at these words.)

136

'I think that the Countess's dress was a little daring for church.'

'She made herself a laughing stock by showing her bust the way she did. What a pitiful bosom. There's only one lady I know who has the right to display such nudities, for they would be at least beautiful ones.'

(Note the pleased glance she gives me. A second punishes me for my temerity, and I become properly timid and abashed.)

'What did you think of the sermon?'

'To tell the truth, I didn't pay much attention to it. My mind was elsewhere.'

'The moral was excellent.'

'I agree, but it was presented in such a cold way. A pretty mouth is always much more eloquent. For example, your words always make such a deep impression on me. They lift me up and encourage me to mend my ways. Alas, you make me love virtue because . . . I love you.'

(My friend, you should see me as I stand before her, quivering and thunderstruck, at my own boldness, I beg her forgiveness. The more she grants it, the more I exaggerate the gravity of my offence.)

My madonna pulls herself together before I do, but I can see that she is still deeply moved. Trying to cover her nervousness, she says that she is going to read me a tract on God's love. Seated opposite her, I run a fiery eye over her meagre body. I turn her statements around, and soon I am reciting Rousseau to her.

This is my opportunity. The chapel becomes a boudoir. I am victorious.

But money! When am I going to get some money? To the devil with it for the moment, and I sent her to paradise with my speculative ejaculation. What bliss she revels in! What delightful nonsense she babbles! How soft and pliant she is!

'Ah, dear Holy Mary! Sweet Jesus!' she sighs. 'My dear friend, did you feel what I did?'

I assure her absent-mindedly that I did, but my thoughts are turned to the damned question of money. I hope you don't think I am stupid enough to have come out on the short end.

I consult with my mentor and I tell him everything. He is discreet, for he would lose too much if he were not. He listens and then tells me he is going to help me. That goes without saying, for he wants his commission.

During the three days. I am absent, my pious friend's only solace is her dildo. The holy man arrives.

'That poor young fellow,' he begins with a mournful shake of the head. 'He has gone back to his evil ways. Abandoned women are dragging him down.'

The news is like a dagger stroke in her heart.

'What a pity, Father. There is good in him.'

'Yes, and it is not his fault. Within him burns the flame of virtue. And he is honest. He confided in me that he has debts of honour which hang over him like the sword of Damocles. If he cannot meet them, I am afraid of what he might do to himself. He said, too, that his greatest regret would be leaving Madame.'

At these words, she demurely lowers her eyes.

The priest pursues his advantage.

'Not only that, but he sighed that although you had his heart wholly, he would have to flee you. Then he

138

pulled his hair, rolled his eyes, and cursed his unlucky star. That is what he said and did, Madame, and there were tears in his eyes. Well, too bad. Let's talk about something else, since there is nothing we can do.'

'But. . . . but, how much do his debts amount to?'

'Three hundred louis.'

Now you can be sure that a woman who has tasted of my lovemaking, who is sure of my discretion, who does not find me a lout, and who wants some colour in her drab life, will send me the sum as soon as she can. Don't you agree?

I see that you are pursing your lips in disapproval. *But that is detestable. Real love is generous and untainted by money. You are nothing but a scoundrel.*

Come now! Don't play the role of a hypocrite. She is thirty-six and I am twenty-four. Although she is still good, I am better. She spends money and I spend my virility. She gets good value, and don't I deserve some compensation?

Moreover, I persuade her to give up her shapeless clothing and straitlaced ways. I launch her into society, which she takes to like a duck to water. She owes me much.

But would it not have been better to leave her in her obscurity? You'll lose her, or somebody will take her away from you.

No matter. I have other plans. Her money is gone, her jewellery sold, and my passing fancy over. But she decides to be faithful to me, and I know she does so just to irritate me. I'll have to behave badly to her. Here is what I have made up my mind to tell her.

'Madame, I shall never forget your kindness, and

my gratitude is nearly costing me my life. The worry I have about your reputation is destroying the happiness I find with you. I have to cease these compromising visits. I realize with heavy heart that with this decision I have signed my own death warrant.'

In the end, her piteous grimaces succeed in weakening my resolve. When she sees that I relent, and my Dulcinea's tears of grief, suddenly hope shines in her eyes. My departure is interupted by halts on every sofa and couch in the house, and I make my escape only at her last ecstatic swoon.

Well, she has made a name for me. No longer do I have to beat my own drum. I just let her sing my praises. In the social barnyard, I am the cock of the roost. You can see that I keep my head about me.

Madame is the intimate friend of the Presidente, a wealthy widow I have had my eye on for some time. She will hear all about me from my rejected mistress, whom I convince to keep up the friendship since it will enable us to see each other now and then. She is so happy that I am not abandoning her just for some Madame So-and-So's beautiful eyes.

Everything goes just as I planned. But now the time has come when I have to make them turn against each other. Discord, heed my voice! There is a little tiff, feelings cool, and the two inseparables hardly ever see each other anymore. The Presidente demands that I side with her, but I lay down some conditions. What a woman won't do for revenge! She surrenders to me just to get back at her old friend.

Although the Presidente is thirty-five, she is well enough preserved to be able to pass for twenty-eight. She could have been a lady-in-waiting if the small talk did not bore her so. She is polite with women, charming with men, and unassuming in public. It is obvious that she is a woman of breeding.

I have never known in a woman such a fiery and sustained passion that changes its colours like a chameleon. Her caresses are all the more seductive because they are sincere. More than once I have been tempted to fall in love with her.

Like most women, she is not without her faults. For one thing, she has a very high opinion of herself. Her decisions are oracular and her views immutable laws. Imperious is the word to describe her. It is true, however, that she does not make it too apparent. More often than not it happens that you are following her dictates when you think you are acting of your own accord.

It is not long before I am lionized by her friends who guess the nature of our relationship. She trusts me implicitly and nothing is right unless I say so. We spend six whole weeks together before I remember that she wants to be privy to all my affairs.

One day, I appear in her boudoir with a downcast mien.

'What's wrong darling. You don't seem your cheerful self?'

(I try to squeeze out a smile.)

'How could I possibly be out of sorts when I am with you?' I bravely say.

She questions me, but I persist in my silence. Even the gaiety at dinner does not drive away the scowl from my face. When we are alone again, I refuse her suggestion of a gambol in bed and take my leave at midnight.

What more do you want, you will ask. Well, I'll tell you.

My lackey, who is as sharp as they come, had the brilliant idea of fucking the maid to pass the time while waiting for me. That evening his appearance is as gloomy as mine. When his sweetheart urges him to tell her what is bothering him, just as mine is doing, he is not so reticent and blabs everything.

'Last night, he dined at Duchess Z's where, in spite of my good intentions, he sat in on a game of faro. His luck was unbelievably bad, and he lost everything he had. He even had to pawn the precious diamond the Presidente gave him. But that was not enough to pay all that he owed, and, as a result, he is absolutely penniless.'

Then he recounts his own woes, for the character is just about as cunning as I am. He took a hand in a game with the other servants, and now all his possessions are in the shop with the three balls above the entrance.

Poor Adelaide, who really loves the rogue, takes out of a drawer forty ecus, her entire little fortune, largely accumulated from the gratuities I had given her. He pockets them without a qualm.

I notice the whisperings between mistress and maid and the stealthy comings and goings. Everything has been told to Madame.

She has my bandit confirm the story and then presses a purse containing five hundred louis into his hand.

Fifteen hundred francs?

In gold, I tell you. It is to pay my debts with a little left over.

When I leave, I find my accomplice already in the coach, and we triumphantly bear home the loot.

You can't be that low.

Of course, I can. And why not?

At seven the next morning, I put on casual dress and hurry to the Presidente. Her eyes sparkle with pleasure when she sees the diamond back on my finger. I try to make her speak. (You remember that my flunky must not breathe a word to me under pain of death.) She lies to me with the most charming grace. But she recognizes from the vivacity of my caresses which are enhanced by gratitude that I am not her dupe. After I am somewhat recovered from my transports, I speak of good deeds. She orders me to be silent. If someone has rendered me a service, I would take away all the pleasure from the benefactor by expression of thanks. My voice wavers.

What a cad you are! You are not touched by so much love and generosity?

Of course I am. To show my gratitude (and to get rid of her at the same time), I marry her off to one of my friends who makes her the happiest woman in Paris. From lovers, we become friends, and I flee, not to new laurels, but to new purses.

Disgusted with ideal love and the methodical passion of the devout and the Presidente, I sadly languish for some time until chance leads my steps to Madame Saint-Just. She is the notorious procuress for elegant orgies at the Rue Tiquetonne. I inform her that I am free and that I am hurting in the purse. She hands me the list of what is available. I scan it.

'Baroness de Conbaille [Yawning Cunt] . . . That's a beautiful name. Who is she?'

143

'A little provincial come to Paris to squander the fifty or sixty thousand francs she had been saving for the last ten years.'

'Is there much left?'

'No.'

'Let's skip her and go on to the next. Madame de Culsouple [Supple Ass]. How much does she pay?'

'Twenty louis a time.'

'In advance?'

'Never. But she's nothing for you. She's too wide.'

'Madame de Fontendiable.'

'Now there is something. An American and rich as Croesus. If you satisfy her, there's nothing she won't do for you.'

'Well, when can you present me?'

'Tomorrow if you wish.'

'Here?'

'No, at her residence.'

The name has a diabolic sound which piques my curiosity. As I return the list, Saint-Just speaks to me with a mysterious air.

'My friend, you have had many younger women, and what did you get out of them? Nothing to speak of. Now listen to the voice of experience. I have here in my house a real treasure. An old woman worth her weight in gold, and with one like her, you run no risk of infection.'

'The devil fuck you.'

'I only wish he would. He's better than nothing. But I am talking about something special. Let me handle it and we'll pluck her together.'

'All right. I'll trust your judgment.'

In the meantime, I appear at my American's the

144

next evening at seven. There I find a vulgar and tasteless luxury along with bales of coffee, sacks of sugar, scales, bills and a pervading fishy odour resembling a not unfamiliar smell.

I am slightly uneasy at the gruff sound of a man's voice in the next room. Her husband? The door opens. Who can it be? It is my goddess! But, damn it, what a woman!

Picture to yourself a colossus of six feet with fuzzy black hair fringing a narrow forehead. Bushy eyebrows set off a certain hardness in her ardent eyes. Her mouth is a cavern. A sort of moustache rises towards a nose stained with Spanish tobacco. Her arms and feet are like a man's and her voice like a klaxon.

'Fuck!' she says to Saint-Just. 'Where did you dig up this pretty lad. He's very young and not my size at all. Well, as the saying goes, little man big prick.'

To get better acquainted, she gives me a bear hug that nearly cracks my ribs.

'Good heavens, how shy he is.'

'He's new at this.'

'We'll take care of that. But did you lose your tongue?'

'Madame, the respect . . .'

(I am still trying to catch my breath.)

'To hell with your respect. Good-bye, Saint-Just. I'll keep the little fucker here. We'll have dinner and a romp in bed.'

When we are alone, my lovely flounces down on a sofa, and without wasting time on preliminaries, I pounce on her. In a twinkling, she is ready to be pillaged. I discover a tawny bosom hard as marble, a

145

superb body, a dome-shaped *mons Veneris*, and a fetching wig. As I caress these charms, she snorts like a bull. Like a mare in heat, her derriere beats the call and her cunt. . . .

My God! I am overcome by a holy frenzy. Seizing her with a vigorous arm, I hold her fast for a moment and then dash on her. It's a miracle. My beloved is tight. With two determined thrusts, I am into her up to my testicles. I bite her and she claws me. Now blood is flowing. Sometimes I am on top, sometimes below. The couch creaks, breaks and collapses, but I am still firmly in the saddle. My strokes redouble in velocity and intensity.

'Keep going, my friend. You're doing fine. Fuck harder. Oh, what bliss. Damn it! Don't pull out. Now it's coming. Get in deeper! Deeper, I say.'

Confound it! She's wiggling her behind so convulsively that I am dislodged, but I hurry to regain. My prick is burning. Grabbing her by the chignon, I return to my former position in triumph.

'Ah, I am dying,' she sighs.

'You slut, if you don't let me discharge, I'll strangle you,' I threaten her.

She is panting more heavily and her eyelashes are fluttering as she begs for mercy.

'No quarter.'

My testicles are in a rage. She falls into a swoon. I pay no attention and withdraw only when we simultaneously emit a flood of fuck and blood.

I think it is about time to put back on her underpants. When we are restored to our senses, my bested opponent gallantly congratulates me. She goes to the bidet. While she is away, I try to put the couch together again.

'What in the world are you doing?' she asks when she returns. 'Don't trouble yourself. My servants are used to that. I have a cabinet-maker who checks it every morning.'

Of course, our conversation is not sentimental. Do you think she can be bothered with such nonsense? We go through her house and to her vault which is chock-full of gold bars. Treasures from the four corners of the globe are assembled here. Finally, we come to a room where she opens a little casket.

'Here, take this wallet.'

'I pretend to be reluctant.'

'Go ahead, you simpleton. Anybody who can fuck like you deserves to be rewarded.'

First ascertaining that it contains five hundred louis in bank notes, I put it in my pocket. It is a generous gesture on her part.

We sit down to a late supper, and I find that I am famished. With her own hands, she serves me morsels, ham stuffed with truffles, mushrooms à la Marseillaise, and for dessert, pastilles so hot that tears came to my eyes. All this is topped with fiery, stimulating liqueurs. From the table, we hasten to her bed where a scene unparalleled in the annals of love takes place.

We make a rendezvous for the next day. I am prompt. Madame is not feeling well. Oh, it is nothing. She is just very hot, and she asks me to open the windows wide, even though it is a bitterly cold January day. Pneumonia carries her off in three days.

Oh woe! I am going to say a *De profundis* for her at Saint-Just's.

After having dried her tears and calmed her nerves, she tells me that my princess had been one of her best clients. In turn, I assure her how deeply shocked I am by this regrettable incident. I add that I have been thinking matters over, and on reflection, since I have always honoured old age, I have come to enlist in the service of the widow she had mentioned.

We take our leave and within eight days I have the honour of being introduced to Madame Methuselah. Since I had been informed that she was extremely wealthy, I am not surprised at the magnificence of the residence and the luxury of the furnishings. I mentally compute how much she might be worth.

I am expected. Before my arrival, I took steps to restore my vitality and charm. In an apparent attempt to repair hers, my hag is still at her toilette. I wait in the lavender and white salon with mirrors and lascivious pictures on the walls. A heady aroma pervades the chamber. Already my imagination is become heated and my heart starts to beat faster. It seems as if fire is coursing through my veins.

The door opens and a young woman presents herself to my eyes. She is simply dressed, which sets off her incredible beauty. This is Julia, the niece of my future patroness. She apologizes for her aunt's tardiness and has come to keep me company if I do not mind.

I gallantly accept her kind offer, but she politely refuses to sit next to me on the divan. My glance follows her as she flutters around the room. I feel love being born in my heart. When Julia becomes aware of my amorous regard, the conversation languishes. But our souls speak.

'Mademoiselle surely must be the comfort of her aunt.'

'I do hope so, for she has been very kind to me.'

'Among the many people who surround her, you must have many anxious suitors.'

Julie's only reply is a deep-felt sigh.

My face turns as red as a beet.

'Monsieur, if you only knew what a worthless lot those admirers are.'

'What!' I exclaim. 'You haven't found one who merits your attention?'

Her voice falters.

'Excuse me. I was going to do something I shouldn't.'

'Mademoiselle, I would welcome it.'

At a sudden noise, Julia's only answer is a significant look.

The aunt has completed her coiffure and makes her appearance.

My friends, picture to yourselves a little girl about sixty years old. Her figure is an upside-down oval. A fiery red wig covers what is left of her hair. Blood-veined eyes regard me in a squint. The lips are tinted a ghastly carmine. From a cavern of a yellow-toothed mouth are squeaked words of welcome.

I notice strings of pearls in the *decolleté* of her black velvet gown. They fall in wave after wave and end where there might have been a bosom forty years ago.

Such is my first impression. It is fortunate that I have not seen or smelt her before.

'My dear boy, I'm so sorry that I had to leave you so long with my niece whom you must have found

149

terribly boring,' she simpers. (Julia disappears.) 'Not many people know that she is my relative.'

'I can't believe it,' I answer in mock surprise.

'Yes, that's so. Her mother was quite a bit older than I.' She clutches my hand and says with a smirk: 'The things Saint-Just has told me about you!'

'She always exaggerates,' I modestly disclaim. 'But I am grateful to her for this opportunity to pay you my respects.'

'Listen, my dear. Let's dispense with ceremony. Relax and I promise you won't regret it. I'm having some people for dinner tonight and I expect you to be one of the party.

My deferential bow of assent is answered by a wet kiss full on the mouth.

(She stinks like a sewer.)

'For the sake of appearances, I want you to pretend that you're my niece's suitor. Pay a lot of attention to her.'

(Heavens, how I would like to make love to that delicious morsel.)

'When the others are gone, you and I can be by ourselves,' she continues.

'So my agony is to be postponed. We pass into the main salon where a numerous company is gathered. While Julia and her aunt are seating the guests, I begin to reflect.)

Love! Love! Again you come to deceive me, lead me astray, break my heart. Cruel deity! Have I not been your victim long enough? Or do you wish to get revenge on me? What role are you going to impose on me? Her beauty and charm will be my torment. She is so desirable, alas! In return for all the incense

I have been burned at your altar, I beg you to spare me. Hear my prayer. A new passion is setting me ablaze. Julia, the lovely Julia, will have my heart and transports while her hideous aunt will have from me only a tribute that she will pay dearly for.

Because everyone is intent on gambling, silence reigns in the room. Julia, at the far end of the salon, is reading a book. In a moment, I am at her side. She is nervous and I am timid.

'Ah, Monsieur, so you have been assigned your place.'

'If you could see in my heart, Mademoiselle, you would learn how dear it is to me.'

'I don't know what you can see in me. I think you are just making fun of me. Besides, it ill behoves you to pay me compliments.'

'So you forbid me? Now, I see. You believe that I am just another of your aunt's employees. I can no longer stand your disdain.'

I stand up as if to go.

'My God, Monsieur, what are you going to do?' she asks in a frightened voice. 'If you leave, my aunt will get suspicious.'

'Mademoiselle, you are right. I am your aunt's lover, but what is wrong with that if it is the only way to be near you? I have been head over heels in love with you for six months now. Have you not noticed how I have followed you everywhere?'

'The poor thing is deeply touched. Her bosom heaves. God! What an admirable and adorable bosom!)

'So you don't answer, Julia. We don't have much time. Quick. Your decision will decide my fate. Do I

151

have to undergo at the same time the favours of your aunt and your contempt?'

'I said the word *favours* in such a mournful tone that the girl could not conceal a little smile.)

'Well, I believe you,' she says. 'Why should you lie to me? I'm so unhappy here, and all I need is for you to make me more so.'

I shall not detail the rest of the conversation except to relate that it was agreed that I would be the aunt's lover and that, affecting indifference for each other, we would meet secretly whenever possible.

We dine. After the meal, the guests start to leave. At midnight, I am alone with my dear aunt who immediately commences to give me an idea of the horrors I shall have to suffer. I grimace at her hands fumbling on my body and face. She goes to her room to get ready for bed while I prepare to join her. Finally, the lover's hour, the fatal hour, sounds. I answer the call, and when I arrive I look everywhere for you know what. I find nothing. Guess where it is hidden. The fat purse is between two candles on Madame's night-table.

My goddess wearing a nightcap is suddenly as desirable as Venus. What charms she possesses! When she smiles at me, I notice that she is no longer able to bite. I finally mount the altar.

Did you have an erection?

Alas, I had to work one up or lose both Julia and the purse. And I desperately needed the latter.

With my hands and feet, I traverse the senile attractions of my Dulcinea. The bosom. There isn't any. Long emaciated arms. A dejected Venus mount. A flabby cunt, whose natural smell is not concealed by the perfume. Closing my eyes and using my imagination, I succeed in stiffening my prick. I get on my old nag and put it in her. She wraps her skinny legs around my neck as I get to the bottom of her. Stretching her neck as I get to the bottom of her. Stretching her neck, she offers me a slimy tongue that I avoid just in time.

Finally, I begin the canter. The old mare is sweating in the harness, but she is returning jab for jab. Her arms go slack and her eyes are rolling. Damn it! I slip out. I am furious. Now I am back in. Things are going smoothly.

'Ah, my friend. My darling. My dearest. I think I am dying. It has been such a long time. Oh, here I am . . . co . . . ming.'

The devil take me. Her convulsions last a full five minutes. She is enjoying herself as a thirty-year-old would. It takes a long time for her to pull herself together. She is absolutely exhausted. I am drenched.

While drying myself, I come across a double wig. It is my hag's that had come off in the scuffle. My beloved is a pitiful sight. She must realize it, for she has a shamefaced look.

'Come, my love, I would like to start all over.'

With that, I spring on her again and acquit myself creditably. Thank God she has taken off her false teeth. Otherwise, she would have chewed me to pieces.

After this second romp, she rings. Mademoiselle Macao comes to repair the disorder of Madame's nightdress and the bed. As I put back on my clothes, the good old woman is praising me to the skies.

'Twice, my dear, just imagine. He did it twice.

153

That fellow is a prodigy. The others were nothing in comparison to him. Just put your hand in here and feel. I am flooded with his sperm.'

It is four o'clock in the morning and I go to the bed to take my leave. After embracing me, she gives me two purses instead of one. She says that they contain two hundred louis, although she normally pays only one.

'No, Madam,' I tell her nobly, 'if I have been happier than the others, I do not expect double compensation. I accept the token of your kindness, but I do not wish to remove the possibility of coming here often and satisfying your desires in a way which seems to give you pleasure.'

She could have taken me at my word, and I don't like to spoil these old bitches. But she is delighted with my response, for she removes from her finger a magnificent ring worth easily two thousand ecus and slips it on my forefinger. Then I part with the permission to come any time I wish and the injunction to appear still in love with Julia in order to conceal our affair. I put up an objection to the latter proposal, but she insists. I yield with poor grace, which pleases her greatly.

Do I find sleep when I return home? No, Julia, your image disturbs me. I see you. I am prey to all sorts of desires. I let out deep sighs. I hear you moaning and accusing me of having betrayed you. Oh, this horrible thirst for money! What makes me squander my essence just for its sake? And it falls on barren ground.

But I am compensated, aren't I. Where would I ever find a more adorable creature than Julia. Dear girl, let love paint me in your dreams and transform the charm of revery into a sweet reality.

Gold! Damn it! Gold. It is the sinews of war. Let the flame of love set fire to my courage and restore my pristine strength which made fall so many virgins under a bloody knife. And you, Priapus, patron deity of fuckers, I invoke your aid. Let me be seized by a lubricious intoxication after I am through with my hag, who I hope splits when I am in her. It would be a disaster worthy of you.

You can imagine that the morning does not pass without my calling on my beloved. Faithful Macao, who admits me, gives me advice on how I can please Madame. I sacrifice to her a pebble of my gold to win a mountain of it. My hag welcomes me cordially. But what a surprise! There is an unaccustomed freshness in her face. The wrinkles are gone. There is colour in her cheeks. If only she had teeth, breasts and hair, she would be eminently fuckable. My hand is frolicsome. My mischievous smile animates her. She orders me to keep my hands where they belong, then she is serious and tells me she has household matters to attend to.

Mademoiselle Macao is Julia's governess. She is understanding. This woman who, in her youth, frequented places where everything is equal, has a sympathy for innocence. She even taught Julia a hand game very popular among Frenchmen.

Now that she is my confidante because of my little donation, she takes me to Julia who is at her toilette.

I don't know why but I become as timid as a rabbit. Her loveliness is stunning. Long ash-brown hair, clear black eyes, and features I would have liked less had they been more regular. We are alone. I kneel down on one knee before her and passionately kiss her hand. Damn it! What has got into me that I am so shy? Julia must be angry. Her modesty must feel repugnant to my caresses. But no. She seems pleased to receive them. She permits the petty larcenies I commit on the peignoir veiling those enchanting globes. I can't keep my eyes off them.

The days pass peacefully by. I gradually make progress with Julia. The aunt overwhelms me with gifts which, I must say, I earn. Then one Saturday, I appear for dinner. My dear aunt announces that she cannot join us, since she has to go out. She will be back only about eight or eight-thirty. It is some charitable function which she never misses. I throw a tantrum. I was so looking forward to being with her. The good woman tries to appease me.

'Don't be so angry, darling. I don't want to leave you, but I have to. But you won't be alone. Julia will keep you company, won't you? She will entertain you on the harpsichord.'

'Yes, Aunt, if you say so,' she answers with a blush. I frown. Mademoiselle Macao is ordered not to let me escape. The hag departs, leaving Julia and me alone together.

The gods above from whom comes this celestial fire which lifts us above ordinary mortals witnessed my bliss. Dear friend, if you want to penetrate into the mysteries of Paphos, read on as you masturbate.

Everything favours my ardour. The beauty of the day, whose rays were softened by a diaphanous drape, add new charms to the objects in the room. It is spring and Julia is innocent, a condition I am determined to change. In glowing colours, I paint the joys of lasciviousness while making protestations of eternal love.

I can see that she is as animated as I. When I touch her, I am positive of it. I get bolder. Already her mouth is prey to mine which is pressed hard to her lips. Her glorious breasts are becoming irritated at the ribbons confining them. Hateful bonds, begone. The tears which are streaming from her eyes I dry with my kisses. Her breathing is laboured. The fires of our hearts and souls become one mighty blaze.

I continue. Julia's arm seems to be pulling me toward her rather than repelling me. Her will to resist is vanishing. Her eyes have a dreamy quality and her eyelids flutter. The treasures I discover and explore!

'Stop!' tender Julia cries in a fading voice. 'How dare you take advantage of me this way? I think I am dying.'

The words expire on the lips of rose. The hour has sounded in Cythera. Eros has waved his torch in the air. Flying on his wings, I battle, and the skies open. I have conquered. Oh, Venus, come to my succour.

Let there be no reproaches for my actions. Julia certainly will not scold me. She wants me to master her and give her pleasure. She expires only to be reborn to taste anew the joys. But a miracle has occurred. Our sofa has come to life. A variety of movements combined with the greatest skill causes a thousand kinds of flowers of voluptuousness to blossom in her heart. Finally, exhausted from the raptures and the caresses, we cease. (And I send away the demon who had lent me his assistance in such an unexpected way.) I no longer recognize the sofa.

When Julie gives me credit for what she has enjoyed, I do not disabuse her of the notion.

I don't stay much longer. My clothes are rumpled. Also, my hag would have a miserly offering.

Without going into boring details, our liaison lasted three months. Julie loved me madly and unthinkingly, so much so that we are discovered. I am given my walking papers and Julie, snatched from my loving arms, is placed in a convent. The Marquise de Vit-au-Conas [prick in cunt] takes charge of the latter affair, and that is how I happen to come to know her.

Interesting herself in me, she asks more information about my affair with Julia. I paint her an accurate picture. Since she is a woman, too, how can she be severe for a crime which is nothing but homage to beauty? She is a friend of pleasure. She learns of my double employ, which, to her, is a good measure of my worth.

'My God!' she says with awe. 'You could have killed yourself.'

Casting modesty to the winds, I tell her that my constitution, far from being enfeebled, is strengthened and requires a job at least as arduous. Her eyes open wide while mine wander. They finally meet. She is no novice, and we soon come to a tacit understanding.

Her service requires her to be often at Versailles, where I go often, also. But at court one is so at loose ends. Her husband is with his regiment and I offer to fill the gap.

During the first days of our liaison, I go one evening to her suite to spend a little time with her while awaiting the King's bedtime. Among the men in the Marquise's circle, I notice a Knight of Malta, a very thin pale man with a haughty air. The grumpy look on the Marquise's face convinced me that he was my predecessor and is about to be given his leave. To help in getting rid of him, I attack him with mockery. But he defends himself poorly.

When I go out he follows me. After the *coucher*, he asks me to accompany him to the park, saying that he wishes to tell me something in confidence. It is a fine night and we stroll until we reach a solitary deserted grove. Suddenly, his hand is at his sword. I grab it and take it away from him and throw it twenty paces away with the greatest composure. He gets angry, but I just laugh at him.

'My dear Chevalier,' I tell him. 'I think I can guess your motives. You were on friendly terms with the Marquise, but now she is throwing you over. It is your opinion that I am your successor, and you are not wrong. You would like to slit your throat along with mine, and I am very grateful for this token of your friendship. However, I'll tell you quite honestly that I shall not fight until I learn if she is worth the trouble. Let's wait until you have had time for reflection and I have been in bed with her. If you still want to after that, we'll amuse ourselves.'

I hasten to retrieve his rapier which I politely hand to him. Then I bid him good evening and go back to my apartment and bed.

The Chevalier comes to me the next day and admits that he was in the wrong. We cordially embrace. Then I repair to the Marquise, who does not look at me unfavourably because of the adventure she has heard about.

The days go by. The Marquise is coquette, playing with my desires perhaps with the thought of awakening true love. We are in the season of little excursions and we see each other fleetingly. I am irritated for time is weighing heavy on my hands. After several earnest entreaties, I obtain a rendezvous for the following day. I can see from the significant look in her eye that it will be all that I want it to be. I appear at the appointed hour. The King is hunting and everybody is outside. The chateau is like a desert. But there are enough people in the Marquise's apartment. Just she. We are alone and our desires gradually increase. On my word, I don't think I've ever had a more delightful companion.

It is noon and the atmosphere in the room is sensuously warm. Occasionally rays of sun appear through the drapes. The chamber is redolent of perfumes and voluptuousness. Picture to yourself on a heap of cushions a tall woman with a fine figure adorned with ravishing contours. Several sashes carelessly tied hold together the flimsy gauze that veils her delightful body. Her bosom is flawless and her eyes are eloquent. The rest of her charms also bespeak invitation.

The preliminaries commence. Without asking her permission. I remove the offending bits of cloth. With two twists of my hands, I have the Marquise in position. I make a rush on her.

My God! I am barely able to hold it back in time. There must be a hex on me. That was a narrow escape.

We assume postures which are mutually agreeable. The Marquise is vivacious without being soft, for hers is a fiery temperament. She truly believes that she is in love with the man in her arms, and once her desires are contented, her heart opens up. Ten years at court can shape a woman. She is skilled in intrigue and dissimulation and seduction.

When strength returns to her, she grabs me with impudence that would have made me blush if one still blushes today. I hold myself back.

'Come,' she says. 'You're just a child. When I first came to live in this country, I was revolted by everything. I was just out of the convent, young and rather pretty. I was bashful and awkward as could be. But women shaped me and men have found me desirable. I won on both sides.'

I live with her as if I am in my own home. We sleep together, and since she finds me extremely virile, she is desirous of keeping me. But the money is not coming, and how does one get it from a woman of the court who is still young and attractive?

The devil provides it.

One day in a delirium, we perform every position described by Aretino in his bible of sex and when we are through, the Marquise takes a fancy for my backside. She insists on doing something with it. I refuse.

'My dear friend,' she begins, 'did you ever see a parrot try to defend its tail against a cunning cat? Well, I'm like that cat.'

'But, Madame, it is a maidenhead.'

'Well, I'll pay a hundred louis for it.'

'Not for all the money in the world. Two hundred. Oh, go ahead.' (I am dying of shame.) Here I am buggered.

The Marquise looks very proud of herself at her

heroic feat. I, with a grimace on my face, am holding my poor wounded behind. But she is so gay that it is infectious and I join her in the mood as she covers me with kisses and caresses.

'Damn it, you nearly killed me, but I forgive you.'

We seal the reconciliation in a way that there is not the slightest rancour remaining.

Good King Dagobert was right when he said that the best of friends have to part. Our liaison lasts six solid weeks. Moreover, I profited mightily from heteroclitoric tastes. It cost her piles of gold.

'Darling,' she tells me one day, 'I can see that we no longer love each other. But I have always liked you, and I hope you will remain my good friend. Nevertheless, let us prevent disgust. You will never want for women. You are young, and I don't want you to waste any precious time. I'll be your guide. For one thing, I'll tell you candidly that the women of the court, and that includes myself, are dangerous beyond words. Nothing is lacking for them to make themselves attractive. Men find in us the manners of good society and the vices of bad. And all these vices are based on one thing, treachery.

'We are flirtish in appearance and depraved in character. Pleasure for us still has its attractions, but we enjoy it out of habit. A new lover is sure to please us. When my husband comes home in the winter, I overwhelm him with my favours, but after twenty-four hours, the illusion of love vanishes. The blindfolds fall from our eyes; we recognize what we really are; and we separate.

'Sentiment is regarded by us as a chimera. We speak of it often and calmly and with interest precisely

162

because we have never been touched by it. You should do well here with your staying powers, your willingness to oblige, and, above all, your talent in the art of lovemaking. I know at least twenty women who would ruin themselves for you, since you would be able to revive their jaded appetites.

'Here modesty is a wry face, decency hypocrisy. Good qualities become corrupt and virtues are tinted with the colours of vice. But fashion and manners cover them. Spirit is appreciated only for the jargon that accompanies it. In other words, fortune depends on us and we are as blind as it is.

'Assume outwardly a bold expression, even impertinent, in a tete-a-tete. Be fast with your affairs and get to the goal quickly. But in public, change your manner. Be as courtly and courteous as you can with the female object of your desires. It is not that we fear indiscretions. We are only afraid of revelations if they are not to our advantage.'

The Marquise stops. Her sofa is not far. There we make our last impassioned adieux. When I leave, I obtain her permission to renew our acquaintanceship from time to time with the stipulation that I not be impaled from the rear again.

A few days later, I run into Madame de Confroid, whom I have had before and who I heard had come into some money. She is petite with a rather nice figure, but there is nothing striking about her face. Although her love grotto is as cold as an icy cavern, she does have a remarkable and extraordinary talent for sucking pricks.

I have never come across any woman even remotely approaching her skill in this art. In my time, I have

163

permitted myself to be fellated by members of the third sex who certainly are no amateurs, but Confroid puts the best of them to shame.

At her coquettish glance, I follow her home where we get into bed. There she sucks me continually for two hours without taking the organ out of her mouth. While she drains me, she masturbates and I fondle her pointed breasts, which is about all I can do.

That is the only way she can get pleasure – sucking a man and playing with herself at the same time. It takes her at least an hour at this activity before she can come to a climax.

I have had normal intercourse with her in every conceivable position without producing any reaction. Once I brought two of my friends with me and we had her simultaneously in all three orifices, but when it was over, she was still as motionless as a rock.

There is nobody like her to get my prick standing up. First she grazes it with her delicate fingers, and then she breathes on it. Her lips wander over my stomach and groin. She nuzzles her nose in my pubic hair, gets close to my sex, teases it with her blowing, and finally gives it a fugitive kiss. She is driving me out of my mind.

When she sees how my prick is throbbing, she knows the precise spot where I am most sensitive. She can judge perfectly the rise of my seminal fluid, for she stops just when I am ready to explode.

After letting it calm down for several moments, her mouth grazes the gland again. She gives it little darts with her tongue. Then her mouth is wide open to take each of my testicles in turn.

Then she quickly turns her attention back to my

virility, running her tongue up and down it, and bestowing little kisses on it. I am trembling through and through and I feel the sperm rising like the mercury in a thermometer on a hot day.

The vixen senses it. She swallows the tip of my prick for just a moment before spitting it out. A second later I would have come. My prick is in agony from this abortive frustrating pleasure, but it is an agony that I could endure forever.

All this time she is masturbating, violently. Furiously her busy fingers open the lips of her cunt as wide as possible. She squashes her clitoris that springs up red and hard and then scratches it with her fingernails.

Because the gland has quietened down, Confroid renews her oral caresses, inserting it in her mouth down to the very bottom of her throat. Again she rejects it just before the supreme moment to pay attention to her own pleasure. Finally, she is becoming aroused.

This succession of suctions sends delicious shivers running up and down my spine. They are a series of voluptuous vibrations which make me shudder like a palsy sufferer. I hear the rattles in my throat.

This time, I think she has made up her mind. The gland is all the way in her mouth. The tip is touching her tonsils while her tongue is all over it.

I can't stand it any more . . . Now . . . I'm coming.

But again the same confounded frustration. With her extraordinary prescience, she ceases her activities a fraction of a second before my ejaculation.

I remain in that suspended state for I don't know how long. I twitch exquisitely with my nerves taut from the interrupted voluptuousness. It lasts interminably.

During one of the pauses, Confroid masturbates even more vigorously. She passes her thigh on my breast so that the cunt with the busy finger in it is only a few inches from my eyes.

She once told me that she had been playing with herself since she was four years old and has been doing it three or four hours every day since then.

While she is thus engaged with herself, I feel the urge to return the homage she plays my sexuality, but she does not let me, saying it would ruin her pleasure. I content myself by stroking her bottom and sticking my finger in her rear aperture.

Waves of passion rush through my nerves, muscles and veins. My entire body is on fire. I fidget and quiver like a woman in heat. I think my organ is going to expire from the raptures.

Suddenly, my whole being is concentrated in a wild torrent rushing across my stomach and through my prick like an unleashed wild river. It is a marvellous fireworks exploding in a thousand spangles that her mouth avidly gulps down.

I am dead from the bliss, but Confroid's persistent suction revives me. She has drunk all my sperm down to the last drop. She is still sucking me. My God! How she sucks me! It is pure ecstasy. I no longer know where I am, perhaps in a sort of coma. The rapture of my prick is my sole sensation. It penetrates my entire being. My mind is a mire of voluptuousness.

I must have a prick capable of eternal pleasure.

Of course, I do not get limp. Fifteen minutes later,

I discharge again, this time even more copiously. Now it is beginning to hurt, but the pain is so delightful.

Indefatigably, Confroid continues to suck while she thrusts her fingers in her cunt more enthusiastically than ever. I see her wrist and fingers dance in a mad twirl. Her irritated hardened clitoris is a purplish blue.

Again I ejaculate. Two times, three times. And each sensation is more rapturous and more grievous. She never ceases her implacable sucking. I clench my teeth in order not to scream.

I no longer have any control over myself. Again I spurt. Writhing in delirious spasms, I think I am going out of my mind. Now pleasure and pain are inextricably blended, and I no longer know if I ejaculate or not. Finally, I am out of sperm.

Confroid is now near the zenith. Her body throbs, her bosom heaves, and her thighs open and close spasmodically.

Now is the time. Brutally I insert one hand in her cunt and other in her rear – three fingers in the vagina and two in the anus.

She gives a convulsive jolt. Finally releasing my lifeless sex, she gives a yelp like a mortally wounded animal. Her body becomes taut, arches, relaxes . . . and collapses. Her screech of rapture is muted and prolonged.

Confroid has reached the climax.

When I take my leave of her, she, knowing my insatiable thirst and need for money, gives me a purse containing a hundred louis.

Here I am free again. I make my way into the various court circles where I cast curious and piercing eyes on the women who are a part of them. Less and less do I keep in mind what the Marquise told me. The season of balls arrives, and I am mad about dancing. But since I am not a blueblood, I am not permitted to take part in the terpsichorean revelries. Nonetheless, being able to watch has its compensations. I have obtained the permission to pay my respects to a spirited and good-hearted princess. I think her just right to inspire a lasting relationship but too intelligent to tie herself down that way. At her age and with her beauty, she would be stupid to do so.

What would Eros say? Has he put his arrows away or is he going to let them all fly on a single heart? Heavens! She is desirable! Perhaps it is possible if I play my cards right.

Now, I am with some gentlemen who express their opinions of the dancers.

'Who is that wild little thing? Her hair is all ruffled, and look at the condition of her gown! But I find her the most seductive creature on the floor. She's absolutely stunning,' I cry.

'That's the Duches of ***,' answers the Count de Rhedon. 'Don't you know her? I'll introduce you. She likes music and I think you'll get along with her.'

The next day, taking the Count at his word, I call on him and we depart.

At six o'clock in the evening, the Duchess is still in her negligee. Long tresses escape from a net on her head. To kiss the Count, curtsy to me, ask me twenty questions, and take me to practise the *pas de deux de Roland* is a matter of only a moment. I am clumsy with the first steps. A lascivious movement makes me bold, gets me all hot and causes me a. . . . How delicious an erection is while doing a *pas de deux*! The Count loudly applauds. She cries that I dance like a god and makes me promise to come often and try out new steps with her. The Count leaves and I remain. She arranges her hair in such a way that I can barely stifle my laughter. When she asks my advice, I arrange it in a coiffure that delights her. She dresses and leaves, and I, too, withdraw.

'She doesn't have the time to be naughty,' I say to myself, as I make my way to bed. Her roguish face torments me all night.

I get up and hurry to the Duchess's at ten o'clock in the morning. She is just getting out of her bath and is as fresh as a rose. A dressing-gown covers from head to toe, but in spite of that, I feel tingles running up and down my spine. After chocolate is served, she leaps up and trips to the clavichord. Her tiny hands run over the keys faster than the eye can see. She has a thin but charming voice. From the expression on her face as she sings, I perceive that she is susceptible.

We play a duet. When I touch her, I soften her in spite of herself. She loses her head and her heart tightens. I hear an almost inaudible sigh. Her voice dies, her hands stop their movement, and her breast rises and falls. My inflamed eye misses not a detail.

All of a sudden, she slaps me on the face, begs my pardon, throws herself face down on the sofa, and then gets up with a great burst of laughter.

Luckily for me, she regains her calm. As we dance, again I happily notice that she seems to be interested in me, for she affectionately praises me. Before I leave, she implores my forgiveness and asks me to impose

169

on her any penitence I might wish. So here I am, an executioner, before this little hypocritical face. I seize one of her hands which I cover with kisses. The other gives me a gentle tap which a bolder kiss makes amends for on the spot.

The following day, I fly there on wings of love. She had asked me to bring some new songs which I have under my arm. She is still in bed. A maid opens the drapes when I appear. Next to her bed an armchair has been placed. I prefer to lean against a console, however.

Where are your brushes, Fragonard, so that I could paint this exquisite child?

A peasant's bonnet half covers her head. Her features have no proportion, but her black eyes are superb. Add to this an irresistible mouth, a retroussé nose, a narrow forehead but piquantly fringed, to or three tiny beauty spots, a peaches-and-cream complexion, and carmine lips that the purest vermilion would not equal.

After an exchange of polite chitchat, I show her the notes. She begs me to sing. I am just getting in voice when suddenly a lifted sheet reveals to me a breast of lilies and roses. My voice quavers, but I continue as best I can. Now appear an arm that must have been fashioned by Love himself, an enchantingly rounded thigh, a well-turned leg, and a dainty foot. I am so intoxicated that I no longer know what I am singing. I am trembling throughout my body.

'Keep on!' she commands in a voice of authority I would not have believed she was capable of.

I start over. My blood is boiling, my nerves are jangling, my heart is beating madly, and my face is covered with perspiration. The little witch is watching me with a malicious smile. One last bound and she is uncovered entirely. Damn! My eyes are bloodshot. Throwing aside the music, I undo the buttons that are constraining me and hurl myself into her arms. She answers my yells and bites in kind, and I leave her only after four vigorous, victorious assaults.

The Duchess has fainted, and when she does not come to, I get a little worried. Consequently, I employ a remedy that has never failed me. My tongue is incredibly voluble. I apply my mouth to the rosebud that surmounts a delightful globe. An involuntary shudder of her body reassures me.

'Dear God! You found it!' she exlaims as she throws her arms around my neck in an ecstasy.

'What did I find?' I ask in some astonishment.

'The passion everybody said I did not have,' she exalts.

Now we are face to face and I assure you that the Duchess is not one of those prudes afraid of a man completely in the buff. As she sensuously wiggles, I discover new charms. A more beautifully formed body cannot be conceived. Fleshy without being plump, slender without skinniness, and a litheness of the thighs which need naught but a little exercise. Her buttocks are bouncing in the air like a performer on a trampoline.

I do like to fuck, but since the Lord in his wisdom did not see fit to grant us the gift of perpetual motion, we have to start sooner or later, for this game exhausts rather than tires.

Now, my duchess has only one jargon, the few words of which she repeats endlessly in a monotonous voice. They become boring uttered in a sing-song voice. How I would like to hear from that purple-rimmed mouth those silly little words that a woman, drunk with voluptuousness, delivers so eloquently. The right expression can render a single caress ever so much more exciting. Now, as one philosopher remarked, ennui yawns with us on the breasts of our beauties. Love vanishes, the swarm of pleasures flies away, and one sleeps the sleep of the dead.

Those are the degradations I have been suffering for two weeks with the Duchess. Our beginnings are so delicious and the endings are so disgusting. Satiety finally wins out.

I am at that point one evening when I am entering my doorway. My servant hands me a jewel-case and a note, which I immediately read:

'An instant rendered me your mistress. Another instant has changed everything. Nevertheless, Monsieur, I am very grateful to you, and I ask you to keep this little case. It contains the image of a woman who once seemed lovely to you and who regrets not having been able to prolong your bliss with her.'

I immediately recognize from which hand this note came. It would have been impossible for the Duchess to have written it. I answer her forthwith:

'Madame, your kindnesses have the right to touch me if your heart has deigned to perceive the littleness of my worth. In our affair, I have exerted an energy which seemed to please you. I am neither spiteful nor bitter. It is enough for me to have had the honours of triumph without even thinking of retreat. For eight days, I have been waiting for your orders, and the

172

proof of my respect for you is not having foreseen them. Your portrait will be for me the token of the esteem you accord to my *talents*. I do hope, Madame, that my successor will bring you more *beneficial gauges*. Both of you will have a very tender obligation toward me, especially when he realizes the price he will have to pay.'

My follower, an intelligent and charming man, was able to last but a few days. After him came a prince, whom she liked for his wit and gallantry, but she had to satisfy herself with his flunkie, the daily bread of a duchess.

Once my reply was finished, I open the case in which I find the Duchess *en deshabille* along with some jewels which were of some value. I take the miniature in my hands. Dare I confess what I did? I make another sacrifice to that pretty robot. The libation pours out over her impish face.

I repair to the residence of Vit-au-Conas, with whom I spent my liberty. Besides, we are good friends. But from the manner in which she receives me, one would think that we were strangers. Soon she warms up and is ready for my tale of woe, about which she had heard something from the Count of Rhedon. She is amused by the catastrophe which I am relating to her when Madame de Sombreval and another woman of equal rank are announced. The latter is attractive and witty and I ask permission to call on her. It is granted.

The visit over, dear Vit-au-Conas says to me: 'So I am going to lose you again, my dear friend. I see that she has designs on you. You are a godsend for her. Act wisely. And dont' forget to push your advantage. Push, push!'

'Ah, Madame, you know that I never fail to do that. Look.' (I make the gesture.)

With my Marquise wishing me good luck, we part, and I rush home to prepare myself for the attack.

Dressed like a dandy and as radiant as a peacock, I hurry to Madame ***. The gathering is numerous. After the preliminary exchange, I examine the assembly. Eight or ten fops pirouetting around, the fawners of the mistress of the house who lean over her and are attentive to her every word, a dozen or so rather coarse women with insolent looks. I am standing with a monsignor, whose income from a bishopric and two abbeys, thought to be a hundred thousand francs, gives him the right to preach virtue to the ladies of easy virtue in Paris and the noble-women at court.

'Do you see that big baroness?' he asks me. 'The one with the flushed face and the porcine eyes with the bristly eyebrows. She is insatiable. Anything that comes her way – coachmen, lackeys, what have you – is her meat. She changes lovers often. Last week alone, she put two in the hospital. She got herself a husband once for lack of anything better, but the poor fellow is now incurably insane.'

'Who is that tall pale blonde?'

'Don't you know the Countess of Minandon?'

'No, but she's tearing her fan to pieces.'

'She's a conceited bitch whom you had better watch out for. Six months ago, she was kind enough to give me gonorrhoea. My prick is still burning. That's what happens when you get out of your diocese.'

He chuckles when I smile at his pleasantry, diocese meaning condom.

'Who is that whispering in her ear?'

'She's the chamber pot for the King's guards. Don't have anything to do with her, either, unless you want to run the risk of syphilis.'

I was going to put more inquiries to him, when someone addresses me and our dialogue is over. The conversation becomes general.

The music hour has come, when Madame *** abruptly addresses me.

'Monsieur, this is your speciality. I know how much you love music.'

'Madame, I am not a musician. All I can do is listen.'

'Well, then,' interrupts the Marquis de Fier-en-Fat, 'you can listen to me. I was born to music. I have a touch all of my own. I am not boasting since it is merely a natural gift. Which devil has bragged about his ears? Now I don't like Gluck. You can't even dance to him. Piccini has no sense of harmony.'

'Monsieur does not like *Iphigenie*?'

'No. It gives me gooseflesh. Now, give me *The Deserter*. That really has an overture. Le Floquet really knows how to compose an opera.'

Madame *** smiles at our little contretemps. When the recital is finished, I prepare to leave, but she holds me back a moment to tell me she would like to see me tomorrow at her toilette.

I have forgotten to describe her. Madame *** is thirty-eight and she makes no attempt to conceal her age. She has a pale complexion and almost transparent skin. Her face is oval-shaped. Her lovely eyes

175

express her thoughts without simpering. A wide mouth. She is rather tall, but the regularity of her curves make one unaware of her height. One thing wrong is her bosom which is small and beginning to sag. It still retains some of its firmness. Although her arms and hands are lean, she has a dainty foot. Even the King has commented on the clearness of her voice. In court circles, she is highly thought of.

Do you have a problem? Her advice is always good. Is a young nobleman looking for a wife? She finds the right girl for him. She knows everything, has experienced everything, guessed everything. She advances her favourites and watches over her protégés. She holds audiences, has a secretary, an office, a treasurer, and there is nothing that goes on which she does not have her finger in.

My God! I'll make my fortune with a woman like that. I am expecting favours. Soon I'll be able to distribute them.

I arrive at the appointed time and am received as an expected caller. While she is at her toilette, we exchange gallantries.

The maids disappear and we are alone. Damn it! I feel this bashfulness again. When Madame sits on the divan, I crouch at her feet. I am very fond of sofas.

'To tell the truth, I think I have made a most extraordinary invitation,' she tells me.

'As for myself, I don't see anything unusual about it.'

'I didn't think you would take liberties this quickly.'

'I think we can come to an understanding, Madame.'

'Whatever are you saying?'

'Simply this. I adore you and my fondest hope is that I do not displease you,' I fervently exclaim.

'I have some plans for you, my dear friend.'

'My only happiness will be to carry them out.'

'You have spirit and fire.'

'Ah, Madame, how could one lack them when one is with you? You would electrify nature.'

She is electrified. Her brow flushes, her eyes sparkle, and her hand trembles. Love, love, come you little bugger.

'That is a pretty dress you're wearing.'

'Since you seem to like the colour, I'll keep on wearing it.'

'What pretty ribbons. They're in the latest fashion.'

'What in the world are you doing?' (I'm untying the ribbons.) 'What would my servants say if they saw you?'

'Madame! We are losing time, time that could be better employed.'

'Suppose somebody came in?'

'So much the worse for the curious.'

My hands wander over her lips and my mouth rests on a breast that heaves under the licking of my tongue.

'Ah . . . Ah . . . You little demon.' Her voice fades. 'I can't resist any longer.'

The hour has come to take my city. I press, squeeze, shove and penetrate. With the second jab, I am in to the bottom. She is around my body like a boa constrictor. Not a movement is wasted.

'Ah, my friend,' she moans 'Not even the Duke can equal you. The Prince would have succumbed by now. The Ambassador never made me discharge so abundantly.'

I wonder if she is going to pass the whole court in review. When we are convinced that there is nothing more to do, we take up our conversation again. Now Madame *** leaves off that haughty air that she affected. I am the fortunate lover to whom she grants all the prerogatives.

Since I can further my career better by inflating her pride, I let her talk about herself. Also, it is in my interest to penetrate into her secrets and intrigues. Never do I lose from sight my ultimate goal – money. The knowledge I glean will help me in my manoeuvres. I realize that my first coup has genuinely dazzled my adorable one. But ambitious women are impervious to real sensuousness, for vanity and cunning absorb all their faculties. Constantly obsessed by envy and hatred, she is poisoned to such an extent that love is impossible. I can only look forward to frigid raptures. I know that I cannot captivate her by playing on her senses, but I can with her vaingloriousness. Also, I know that in sexual matters her views are limited. My plan, therefore, is to subject her to me, to master her, to make use of her fortune, or to get rid of her if she serves no purpose.

As a rule, all I need is a fortnight to gain my ends. By that time, I have been able to twist Madame *** around my finger. She adopts my ideas in the belief that they are her own. I know her thoughts without her knowing mine. That is not all. She has business affairs which I intend to run. All I have to do is suggest it, and she turns them over to me. I make deals, sign contracts, and pay myself a salary without any objection on her part. My only guide is my conscience.

I am too intelligent not to remain in the background. Madame *** is still in titular charge and also takes the brunt of my mistakes. That is the sign of a crafty man. Before telling the final catastrophe, I want to mention two or three incidents that are somewhat out of the ordinary.

The world-famous Abbot Ricaneau had been asking for donations for some time. He has a good income, but the good Abbot, possessed of the virtue of proliferation, regularly produces four infants a year. Being not without a conscience, he pays the salary of the wet-nurse before enriching the collection of the foundling home. Someone suggested our office. He comes to see me, and I thought his request reasonable. But I demand a detailed report, which he brings the following day. With a smirk, he tries to bribe me with a purse whose thinness makes me knit my brows.

'Monsieur,' I tell him. 'I assume that these are just for the incidental expenses such as the gratuities to the porter, nurses and secretary.'

The Abbot does not dare contradict me. I look at the report carefully and discover several difficulties. He begs my help to overcome them.

'You have to make up your mind,' I say. 'You want an abbey with an income of twelve thousand livres. Since you are one of my friends, you can have it for a mere thousand.'

He expostulates. 'What!'

'A mere trifle, and I am disappointed in you.'

When I go out the door, he follows me like a dog, screaming and yelling. But I outshout him, threatening to tell one and all about his scandalous offer. I mutter something about *lettres de cachet*. At that, he makes his escape, leaving me with the purse, which I find held a miserable hundred louis.

A few days later, a very attractive woman is ushered into my office. Her request is a lieutenancy for her husband, who had served in the army for twenty years and had suffered several wounds in battle.

Do you think that I spoke with the voice of generosity? Well, you are not mistaken. I make several gestures to her signifying my benevolence. At first, she is very shy, but I soon win her over. Then we are chatting like old friends. In less than an hour we are one flesh.

Did you fuck her?

No, I turned her over to someone else. God, what a fool you are! She was one of the best I ever had. For a woman from the provinces, she showed real talent.

At least you got some money out of it.

That goes without saying. I have her write her husband to deposit ten thousand livres to my account. In exchange, I give her a gold ring some scoundrel presented me with that morning to enlist my help in getting him knighted. It was worth about twenty-five louis. You see how generous I am. It was more than the interest on her investment.

Our business is going famously. Under my skilful management, dross turns to gold. Madame *** adores me. Of course, she sleeps with everyone, but I am her favourite because I hold the purse-strings. At times, I feel pangs of conscience, but she soon cures them.

Now here is what happened. There was a lovely young woman, very wealthy, who had only one lover.

And who was he?

Her husband. There are still some eccentrics who believe that their wives should only sleep with them. She naturally thought he was out of his mind and had him locked up. She came to me to help in arranging the formalities. We saw to it that he had an income of six hundred francs a year and that he would be dressed decently. Madame *** and I fixed a fee of ten thousand ecus, which was a bargain. Eight days later, officials took the lunatic, shaved his hair, and led him off to the asylum.

We thought that the matter was finished. The wretch was supposed to have rotted away or at least have become insane. But he had the devil in the flesh, for nothing of the sort happened. A certain magistrate happened to visit the asylum where our inmate told him his story. The official was sympathetic and believed him. He informed the minister, who immediately preferred charges against Madame ***. She was found guilty, heavily fined, and went to bury herself in her estates in the country.

My dear friend, do you think that I was going to hang myself? Of course not. I just went to count my money. I found I had twenty thousand ecus plus quite a bit of jewellery. But I was sorry about the fate of the poor woman. I could have got much more through her. I wondered if I should pay my debts. Oh, I decided not to worry about that. Why should I give those usurers anything? They've always sucked me dry before. They could wait for my will or marriage. In short, I made up my mind to seek new fields.

There was a fête in which the town and the court participated. I cast my eye on the assembly and the alluring faces therein. Oh Satan, get thee behind me.

Already I felt my face lighting up and my pocketbook being emptied. With great fanfare appeared Madame Cul-Gratulous, who because of her position, felt she had to attend the festivities. That was the only reason, for she would never go to public places to seek her pleasures.

Remembering me, she invited me into her box. It certainly was not her figure which tempted me. Her head, neck, torso and derriere were all one piece. Dowdily dressed. Fat arms with varicose veins. Thick thighs and bowlegs. Squint eyes out of focus. A moustache stained with tobacco. Her head was topped with a tousled wig. She was adorned with diamonds, ribbons and fluff. That will give you an idea of the physical appearance of the Countess.

What about her morals?

Fuck. Let's not talk so loud. You realize that she is a grande dame. Every time she walks by, her servants kowtow. She terrorizes her husband, her father, and even her grandfather. But she does not have overly high aspirations, for fear she fall too far. For the rest, she is malicious, peevish, shameless, vulgar and opinionated. She thinks that she is the soul of generosity when she hands out her coins.

But what do you think you are going to do with a monster like that?

What am I going to do with her? That's a fine question. I am going to plunder her and swallow her up while I fuck her.

The spectacle finished late, and she invited me to have dinner with her in a tone that was almost an order. I pretended that I was overwhelmed by the honour.

The meal was formal and consequently dismal. One ate little and spoke less. As we began to file out, a valet whispered to me that Madame wished to speak to me before my departure. He added that I was destined to spend the night with her.

Mademoiselle Branlinos, the Countess's personal maid, greeted me at the bathroom where she said she had orders to prepare me.

'Heavens, I never expected such cordiality, Mademoiselle, but do with me that you will.'

We entered the bathroom, but I was hesitant about appearing completely nude before Mademoiselle Branlinos, who was helping me off with my clothes. She was a delightful thing, not more than twenty.

'Hurry up, Monsieur, I have to get you ready.'

Ripping off her clothes and the last of mine, I fucked her on the rug of the bathroom. She was not displeased and I was amused by the game. But we had to think of my bath. We both got into the tub, Branlinos mentioning that I had dirtied her. She also said that she would form the third of the trio for the evening.

When we were thoroughly washed, dried and anointed, she nimbly escaped my grasp, fearing, she said, another pollution. Five minutes later, she came to fetch me.

I entered the bedroom. The Countess was already in her couch. She extended me a hand which I kissed with as much ardour as if she had been pretty. I sat on one side of her and Branlinos on the other. Although Madame was a little more human, decorum still prevailed.

'My dear,' she said to Branlinos, 'see if he has an erection.'

As soon as the petite touched it, it sprang up like a soldier standing at attention.

'Oh, Madame,' she cried. 'It's as hard as an iron rod.'

At that, Madame Gratulos turned around and presented me – guess what?

What?

You certainly are stupid.

I'm sorry, but I don't have the faintest idea.

Her derriere.

Her derriere?

Yes, her backside, an enormous mound of sagging flabby flesh.

I immediately went soft at the sight, but Branlinos resurrected me. When she opened the entrance to the abyss, I gritted my teeth and began to do my duty like a man. I was in the midst of doing what I doubted I could do while Branlinos was masturbating the old cow. During my fucking, I was sweating through every pore. The moment of discharge was nearing. Did you ever hear the sound of a squeaky gate with rusty hinges being opened? That was exactly how my lovely released her load.

When the ordeal was over, she had the kindness to give me a wet kiss. Damn it! I preferred the other aperture because it did not smell so bad.

After an interlude during which we conversed, I had to perform the same ritual. Never have I felt more ridiculous. Nevertheless, I acquitted myself valiantly.

'Would you like to fuck Branlinos?' my future patroness suddenly asked me.

I jumped at the proposal. Suddenly, I felt myself being rummaged. Her finger was all the way in the most shameful part of me. So that was why she let me fuck the little one, so that the pill wouldn't be too bitter to swallow. Cul-Gratulos left off only when I was groggy with fatigue. Dawn was breaking when I withdrew. I was made to promise to keep the goings-on a secret, and I have faithfully kept my word.

The following days were marked by the same adventures. The gold she showered on me was sufficient compensation. But if it had not been for Branlinos, an erection would have been out of the question.

When my term was finished, she left to take the waters at Vichy, loading me with farewell gifts with her haughty air, and I went back to Paris.

Back in Babylon which has the most corruption of any city in the world simply because it has the most people, I wore myself out paying calls on every coquette and scoundrel in Paris. For more than two weeks nothing eventful happened. I was bored to tears, I gambled and lost. I saw that my sustenance would be gone if I continued, and so I considered flight to avoid the temptation of the tables It was a momentous decision which I carefully weighed.

Already the sun was gilding the crops and the Graces were retreating to the copses. And all the women were flying to the countryside. Their example decided me and I followed them. You can be sure that like a busy bee I sucked only the juiciest blossoms. Nevertheless, it was tedious.

You know as well as I those enchanted palaces that

line the shores of the peaceful Seine. I went there and found nothing.

Finally, I went to the Marne where rise walls built by our forefathers. Their imposing aspect seems to proclaim that kings reside there. But no. It is merely the abode of the brides of Our Saviour, the convent of ***, whose abbess is the aunt of one of my acquaintances. She has been told that I am likeable and I am welcomed with open arms. You have no idea of the excitement I cause when I arrive. The pretty little nun coquettishly adjusts her wimple when she sees me. All rush to the visiting room.

When Madame Abbess appears, all vanish out of respect. What a voluptuous figure she has. I could almost eat her.

She has just reached her fifth lustrum. To the flower of youthfulness is joined the blossom of perfect health. A glittering face with eyes blacker than jet, a rose-bordered mouth, and teeth of ivory that she permits me to admire. There is something of the flirt about her which her garb cannot conceal.

When she notes the lust in my eyes, she says to me teasingly: 'Are you another Abelard?'

I don't know what to say. But I know that I am going to fuck my Abbess or know the reason why. The compliments we exchange are prettily turned on her part and gallant on mine. Soon we are chatting as if we had known each other for years. My God! Now I have an erection that is killing me. It is the result of gazing too intently at those seductive breasts.

I shall not speak of the parties that were given in my honour or the recitals. There could be heard my sonorous male voice blending with the titters of the timid novices. A satyr is loose among captive nymphs, in effect. In vain do they try to flee, but there is something about me that stops their steps. As they totter, the squeals they emit are not those of fear.

What a wonderful thing to find yourself in a seraglio of twenty little nuns who vie with one another in loveliness. Their eyes reveal a tender languor. Several of the innocents have twitches they have never before experienced. How sweet they look. Let's fuck. Let's fuck. Oh, my prick, show what you are capable of. Hail Venus! Hail Priapus!

Contemplating such matters, I toss about in my bed. I am unable to sleep because of my excitement.

The next day, Madame the Abbess is slightly indisposed and keeps to her bed. I receive permission to pay my respects in her apartment.

What has come over me? She is as lovely as an angel. I forget why I have come. She extends her hand to me as she asks about my health. With passion I kiss that hand. She gives a sigh. Another sigh is my response. We are alone. Her half-closed eyes, her fluttering eyelashes, the distension of her stomach, and the palpitation of an alabaster bosom still covered by an inopportune veil embolden me. 'Julia! Julia!' Such are the first sparks of our fires. I kneel at the side of the bed with my burning lips on the hand that I did not relinquish. She makes no attempt to snatch it away. Heavens! She has fainted. She is dying. I summon her servants with screams of terror. Salts, waters, scents!

'That's one of Madame's dizzy spells,' cries one of the maids.

But it is not her final attack. After a quarter of an

hour, she returns to her senses, pale as a sheet. Her pallor, however, is that of a woman in love. Several tears have dampened her beseeching eyes. Finally, we are by ourselves again.

'I apologize for these attacks which nearly kill me. The doctors cannot seem to diagnose them.'

I note the colour returning to her cheeks. Her pulse becomes normal. My heart is pounding as I approach her. Several disarranged pillows offer me a pretext. As I advance my hand to straighten them and hold her up – oh wonder of wonders! – her opulent bosom is offered to my view. The sight intoxicates me. I press my amorous mouth against her amorous mouth. My tongue gives her quivers of voluptuousness. Gradually, I make my way to the sanctuary. A finger penetrates it. It gives a twitch, one which excites her still more. What ineffable bliss!

'Sweet Jesus!' she moans. 'I can't stand this wonderful feeling. I think I am expiring.'

The sensations are too much, too new. Unable to withstand the shock, I sink back in a faint. She is worried to such an extent that she rings for her maid. When I come to, I find myself in their arms. Their efforts to revive me are so successful that the petite maid, on seeing the condition I am in, deems it wise to retire. The Abbess and I reiterate a thousand times our vows to love each other eternally, and after each oath, we seal it with the appropriate ceremony.

I am nourished with the strongest broths and foods. I spend the day as I did the morning, and the night is just as joyful. The following days, diversions without number are prepared for me – hunting, fishing and games. Such thoughtfulness strengthens my ties to the

Abbess even more firmly. She is lascivious without being coarse. She takes my advice and my lessons inflame her. Her lovely svelte and flexible body and her shapely legs enlace me, melt into my body. Only in my arms does she enjoy repose.

I would have been true to her, but the flesh is weak. Young hearts are pining for me, and should I let them wither and fade away? No, I am too compassionate.

I establish a schedule – my nights are with the Abbess and my days are occupied otherwise. The dormitories and cells are all open to me, and I take advantage of it. The first one I fuck is discreet.

Discreet? You must be joking.

I am not. It is with the maid who restored me. And that's the truth. She was in charge of my meals. One day, I was so excited by the chase that I return late. She is not expecting me. I enter her cell. Guess what meets my eyes.

She is sprawled out in a big armchair with her robe lifted up to her navel and her legs spread wide apart. With a great deal of enthusiasm she is manipulating – a dildo!

I shut the door quickly. Precipitately, she drops her petticoat and leaves the spear in the wound. With a deep blush, she stands up and starts to walk away with her thighs squeezed closely together. The devil inspires me. Taking her under the arms, I free Priapus who soon finds refuge deep in the centre of the comfortable chamber. She makes a feeble protest.

'My dear, I caught you in the act. And I am going to finish what you started. Don't worry. I won't betray you.'

I lay her on the couch, where I perform the sweet task twice.

'God bless you,' she sighs when it is over.

One day, the Abbess beckoned me and led me to a cell. Putting her finger to her lips, she pointed to a peephole and motioned me to have a look through it. I did as I was bid and saw Sister Stephanie in the adjoining cubicle.

Dear Sister Stephanie — such a romantic name. Young, rosy cheeked and ash blonde, she reminded me of a bouquet of flowers with her gentle charming voice and her veiled look which seemed to conceal so many tender secrets.

And the cell. It was a weird world, a bizarre enclosure whose walls were not limed with white but with blue, a sky blue that was almost ethereal. The ceiling, too, was painted with the same azure while the floor was of carefully waxed white planks. The bed looked comfortable.

What was out of place in the nun's cell was a Christ nailed to an oversized cross bracketed to the wall, but the figure was not that of the emaciated Saviour that is so familiar. He was a robust male with powerful pectoral muscles. Moreover, the body was made of a material with an astonishing resemblance to human flesh. I saw Stephanie touch it and her finger sank in.

As for the face of the Christ, the expression was one of ecstasy, a profane rapture that had absolutely nothing to do with religious exaltation. It was a handsome face, masculine and virile. The nostrils and lips were sensual, and there was a glitter in the eyes.

The door opened and in stepped Angela, one of

the more delicious of the novices, who was warmly welcomed with a kiss.

'What lovely hair you have,' Stephanie remarked.

'And how about yours, Sister Stephanie?'

'I am rather vain about it.'

'But I thought when you took your vows, you had to have your head shaved.'

'Yes, you do. But if you get on the good side of the Mother Superior, she gives you permission to let it grow and fix it any way you like. It goes without saying that you can't let it show. Certain nuns would understand these special marks of favour.'

'Show me your hair,' Angela demanded.

Without any hesitation, the woman removed her wimple, and a cascade of tresses tumbled down over her shoulders. Silky curls, elegant waves fell on the white starched collar that formed a part of her costume.

After a gasp of unfeigned admiration, Angela asked permission to brush it.

The girl sat down facing the sister and began to brush the hair with measured strokes. Suddenly, Stephanie kissed Angela's lips with her moist mouth. At first, the girl shrank back but then surrendered her lips and tongue. In a trice her body was embraced. I could see that her sex was being ignited. The sensation must have become even more unbearable when Stephanie caressed the yearning breasts through the blouse. Then, baring them, she took the nipples in her mouth and sucked them slowly and avidly.

'I think I have wet myself,' Angela murmured.

Finally, Sister Stephanie disrobed, exhibiting her nude body with arrogance and hauteur. She possessed opulent round breasts, a thick fleece, smooth thighs, and delicious buttocks.

With deft nimble hands, she quickly divested the girl of her clothing, pushed her back on the bed and began to fondle her ardently.

I could see that Angela had lost touch with reality and I surmised that this was the first time she was experiencing true voluptuousness. Her twitches soon became violent convulsions.

She sank back in a faint from the force of the sensations. But she recovered under the tingling caresses that the sister was bestowing between her open thighs with her agile darting tongue. Then I heard the enamoured sighs, the squeals of joy, and the prolonged moans of pleasure which announced the arrival of the supreme sensation.

They fell back in exhaustion, but I kept my eye glued to the aperture. After a few moments, Stephanie rose and left the bed. I followed her with my eyes as she went to the Christ, pressed herself to it, embraced his muscular thighs, and licked his face. Now she stepped back and began undoing the loin cloth. When it dropped down to the floor, I observed to my astonishment that crucifixion did not necessarily cause loss of virility. And what virility! It was a long member which swayed and vibrated, a foully attractive object the like of which I had never seen. Although it was monstrous, I found it strangely attractive, and I could recognize that this organ nestled between hairy bloated sacks could promise a woman certain raptures.

Stunned with amazement, I watched Sister Stephanie slowly impale herself on the colossus. As she let herself slowly down it, she shuddered and gave little groans. Now she slowly jabbed herself with it in a regular cadence. The cheeks of her buttocks were tightly closed to augment the sensation.

Now the nun began an almost motionless dance which ended with a loud shout followed by a long obscene rattle.

Let's pass over in silence several rather ordinary incidents. I fucked Sister Lapine, Sister Magdelon, Mother Bonaventure, etc. The dormitory, the garden, the dispensary and the chapel are all the theatres of my exploits. But let's discuss the novices.

They are five, and among them, Sisters Agatha, Rose and Agnes stand out. They are the most adorable creatures imaginable. The first two are inseparable and play with each other for lack of anything better to do. Agnes is in love with me, but she hides her feelings and weeps to herself. One day, I find the means to share her room with her.

'What's wrong with you, Agnes?' I demand of her.
'I really don't know.'
'For the last week, something has come over you. You are completely different. You used to laugh and be so much fun, but now you just look out into space and sigh. Tell me what's wrong. Or don't you trust me, who loves you so much?'
She flushes. 'You do love me? If only that were so.'
'Have I offended you?' I ask, taking her hand.
'Please leave me. I don't feel well.'
She rises.
'I see that you are afraid of me. Perhaps I am hateful to you. I think it is about time for me to leave.'
'You're not going?' she cries.

193

Poor child. She's mine. No further effort is needed. I shall soon have her.

The head of the novices provides me with a good opportunity a few days later. You will recall that she is a good friend. The choir is supposed to sing a motet, but the music-master does not come, and so she confides Agnes to me for the rehearsal.

As soon as the good sister closes the door on us, I resume my attack: 'Lovely Agnes, are you always so cruel?'

She lowers her eyes.

'How unhappy I am. Only God knows how much.' She raises her hands to heaven.

'Agnes, you have made tears come to my eyes.'

'What do you think about me. I have been crying my heart out.'

Her tears fall fast and heavy.

'Let us console each other. If we don't, I shall die.'

'No,' she sobs. 'You cannot die. It is I who shall have to.'

I take her and put her on my knees with her head against my face.

'Agnes, it is only you whom I love. Tell me that you love me. too.'

'You wicked man, how can you have any doubt about that?'

Her mouth grazes my lips. The girl does not recognize the significance of the outbursts of her heart. Her hour is come. I cover her with kisses. I transfer into her heart the fire that is devouring me. I make her drunk with caresses and kisses. When I remove the last of the veils, I am stunned by the treasures that are revealed. Modesty no longer holds me back. She

194

no longer knows what she is doing. Like a flash of lightning, I strip her bare. The scream that Agnes lets escape is the signal of my victory.

You are probably thinking, fool that you are, that she makes a painful face and puts on airs and that she is despising me as her rapist. On the contrary, she thanks me from the bottom of her heart, the poor child. It is true that I merit the praise, for the fortress is damnably difficult to take.

Afterwards we begin work on her part in the motet. When the Mother Superior returns, Agnes is singing with the voice of an angel. As for myself, I am scorched and scalded. But twelve hours of repose heal my scars.

What a way to spend your time.

What do you mean, you fault-finder?

I'm scolding you because you are wasting your time without getting any money.

Oh, I forgot to tell you that the Abbess was the soul of generosity. No woman has ever been so bountiful. Now that your fears are calmed, let me continue with the account of my exploits.

Sisters Agatha and Rose are deserving of my homage. The elder cannot be more than eighteen. The former, possessed of an irrepressible spirit, has the devil in her flesh. Rose is more thoughtful but gay at the same time. These two girls are united by a mutual understanding. The Abbess, whose jewels they are, told me in confidence that more than once she allowed them in her bed to appease their desires. The excesses they gave themselves up to! When I give them dancing instruction, we do all sorts of silly things.

'Sisters,' I say one day, 'would you be good enough to show me the games you play with each other.'

'What games?' demands Agatha as Rose blushes.

'If I knew, I wouldn't be asking you.'

'Well, Rose, I think he means hide-and-seek.' She begins to giggle.

'There's nothing hidden,' I tell them sternly. 'I saw everything.'

'What?' asks Rose in consternation. 'You saw? Agatha, we are lost.'

Both begin to weep.

'Dry your tears,' I order them. 'I promise I won't say a word.'

That reassures them somewhat. Besides, what they have done is considered in a convent only a little sin.

'But how were you able to spy on us?' Agatha timidly asks me.

'I really didn't see you. A little genie told me what you were doing.'

'A genie?' she exclaims.

'A genie?' echoes Rose.

'Yes, a genie who comes to me every day.' I can barely stifle my roars of laughter. 'I'll introduce you to him on the condition that you teach me your game and that you listen to what he has to say.'

'What? Does he speak, and how?'

'We talk to each other in sign language. I'll explain later.'

'Let's see.'

'Yes, let's see,' chimes in Rose.

'Easy,' I warn them. 'Wait until I summon him. In the meantime, perhaps you would like to show me your game. . . .'

(I had my reasons, but never has my jinni been so recalcitrant. I did my best to spur him to action, but nothing occurred. Finally, the imp arrived. Here is what happened. I produce the Monsignor, which makes Agatha's eyes pop. She springs towards it.)

'Oh, Rose, I have it in my hand. Look at how beautifully it is fashioned. But it doesn't have any nose!'

'Help me to hold it lest it fly away.'

Rose clutches it.

'How quickly it came.' She tries to unhinge it.

'Young ladies, just a moment. Don't you see that it is just a little snail. It's in its shell.'

'That's so,' Rose says. 'Look at it in its cushion.'

'I've never seen a snail like this one,' Agatha comments.

'It's probably from China.'

'Where are its feelers?'

I am dying of fear lest I should be emancipated in their tender hands.

'I think he wishes to speak,' I tell them.

'We would like to hear him,' they reply.

'I have to warn you that if you get him angry, he will go away and never return. Now, mum's the word.

I grasp Agatha and throw her on the bed. She is a brave little thing, not uttering a word. In a moment, I have her skirt up to her waist. Wild with curiosity, Rose flutters around.

'Agatha, is he speaking?'

'Oh, yes. I have never heard such eloquence. I don't think I can stand it any more.'

'What is he saying?'

It goes without saying that she has other things to

do than reply. The little she-devil wiggles so divinely that I am about to begin all over again, when Rose, unable to contain herself any longer, grabs me. The overheated perspiring genie emerges from the carnage and begins to work on Agatha's companion. Although she is not as vivacious, she is almost mad with voluptuousness. But she has that rare quality I have always appreciated in a woman — the door of the sanctuary closes after the sacrifice without leaving me time to go limp. By now, neither of them is plying me with questions. They are in a state of utter ecstasy. As for myself, I take keen enjoyment in their confusion. We no longer speak of the game. They realize that they have been fooled, but they hold me no grudge.

I am at the peak of bliss, although somewhat fatigued. Every time I consider giving up the game, the devil comes out of his hiding-place and spurs me to new efforts.

Life becomes heaven and hell. You remember that three goddesses fought for one apple. Well, imagine what it is like when twenty little eager nuns compete for one man.

My friend, you have no idea of a female republic whose doge is the Abbess. The majority of the girls have been enrolled in the celestial militia against their wills. Although they are the wives of an ethereal being, they still have corporeal desires. The result is a charnel revolt, a conflict between the senses and reason, between the Creator and the creature. All that stimulates the passions, irritates desires and inflames imagination. That is why the girls get spasms and nervous attacks. They can't be praying all the time.

The normal object of their adoration is the confessor. If there are two, they share the fold, each hating the other cordially. If there is only one, the lambs fight amongst themselves for his favours.

'What! Over an old monk?'

'Yes. Over an old monk. They would do anything for him, for at least he is of flesh rather than wood or metal.'

Consequently, in these abodes of peace and innocence, one enjoys all the comforts of hell.

If only you knew the ruses the girls employ to sneak their lovers over the walls. I could tell you of the horrors of the despotism the vicious old women wield over their charges. There take place orgies worthy of being described by Aretino. When they are married, they have been initiated into every vice imaginable.

The murmurs of discontent are becoming louder. The governing body holds a session. Fault is found with the Abbess who demands that her tastes and pleasures be respected. The reverend mothers are all ears as they eavesdrop. The little innocents are trembling with fear. The way they all look at me leads me to believe that I'll be the scapegoat. For fear of losing me, the Abbess stoutly defends me. The complaints are brought to the attention of the Bishop and thick-witted priest, who announces that he is coming in person to restore order in a house into which Belial has insinuated himself. I am ready to face him, but my dear Abbess persuades me that if I stay, she will be ruined. Loaded with sugar and gold, I make my departure. There is scarcely a dry eye when I leave.

I stop in Paris just long enough to deposit my loot and then proceed to Picardy to finish the season. I do not stop in the provincial capitals where the vices are the same as in the capital with the difference being that they are cruder and more ridiculous.

The friend I am staying with has a rather large estate where the hunting is excellent. The mansion is venerable and imposing. His wife is lovely and he holds his years well. But they are Philemon and Baucis. It is not that she is devout. No, she likes a joke, and she gladly receives gallant advances for she knows how to take them. When I am with her, I feel nothing but admiration and respect.

Monsieur and Madame d'Obricourt live amicably together with her husband entertaining no suspicions. Nevertheless, Madame has a lover with whom she mocks her spouse. A rash act destroys the complacency of Monsieur. While everybody is out hunting, I am alone in the house with Madame. She goes to her boudoir to write some letters while I remain in the salon reading a book. Suddenly, with a missive in her hand, she goes out. Her husband, unexpectedly returned, enters at the same moment.

'Ah, Monsieur,' she says. 'What is wrong with you? You are as pale as a ghost.'

He turns his face to the mirror. Unfortunately for her, I am reflected in my entirety and he sees her slipping me the letter which I do my best to hide. He is seized by an attack of jealousy. Before I can gather my wits about me, I am facing a rifle. 'The letter or your life.'

'You're out of your mind,' I retort. 'Even if I have one, it is obviously not intended for you and you have no right to it.'

'I do not need your advice,' he tells me coldly. 'The letter, or you'll have a bullet in your body.'

I have no choice. I get up, give him the envelope, and shove Madame into the study for she was stupid enough not to have budged.

The perusal of the letter gives the husband more information than he would have liked to have. He realizes that he is a cuckold. Under his phlegmatic exterior, he is a man of violent emotions. The other guests who have come back from the chase do not notice anything wrong. Monsieur uses the same terms of affection when talking with his wife. I cannot get over it.

I have always been suspicious of concealed anger, and I am not wrong this time. Finally, one morning, he finds her in her bedroom with some other women, wives of friends, and beats her within an inch of her life. Unaccustomed to such treatment, she leaves to go to her mother-in-law who has a weakness for her. The old woman is a Jansenist who has little liking for her son because he does not share her views on the after-life.

Madame is aware of this, and on the basis of this knowledge, she lays her plans.

'Mama, I have come to throw myself in your arms,' she says. 'For more than a year now, I have been suffering the tortures of the damned. And it is all because I am a Jansenist; and he has no use for them. He has been mistreating me terribly. He got his hands on a letter I wrote to a priest who was giving me instruction in this belief. And then he accused me of having an illicit affair with this man of God. Now he has been beating me. These ladies are my witnesses. I don't know where to turn except to you.'

Tears stream down her cheeks as the ladies nod their heads to back up her story.

'What a scoundrel and blackguard!' exclaims the mother-in-law. 'My daughter, you will stay with me and I'll take charge of things. If he is rash enough to try to do anything to you, I'll. . . .'

It is necessary to get the letter from her husband's hands. The old woman orders her son to send it to her immediately, or he will be disinherited within twenty-four hours. He knows his mother, and he is not about to forfeit an income of forty thousand livres. There is no choice but to obey. He sends it but with a note of explanation. It is in vain. The mother-in-law turns everything over to Madame, who throws the envelope and its contents into the fire.

The furious Obricourt calls me up as a witness. I say that I don't know anything. Yes, I had a letter, but I was ignorant of its contents. That is not the end of the matter. There is a separation. The old Jansenist dies, leaving her daughter-in-law an inheritance of twenty thousand livres a year.

Tired of shooting hares and bored with the company of the landed gentry, I take refuge on the banks of the Somme. There, an old chateau dating back to the twelfth century is now the home of owls and bats, or at least, it seems that way. But, in reality, it is the abode of an old cantankerous baron. Because of his geneaology, he does not have to have intelligence.

As the old song goes, the Baroness yearns to have someone clean her flues. The Baron, who cannot, does not wish anyone else to perform the task. It is to do this charitable work that I come. I heard that he is rich as Croesus, and in order to part him from some of his wealth, I am ready to suffer his boring conversation and coarse manners.

I am not given a cordial welcome. When he observes that his wife pays me little attention, he becomes warmer. I bring him numerous greetings from mutual friends in Paris, and while he is going through them, I observe the belle.

She is a piquant brunette with a tawny complexion. Her lovely black eyes sparkle lasciviously. Her teeth are like pearls set off in a frame of carmine lips. The bust is slightly too big for her delicate figure. She cannot be more than twenty. All in all, she is eminently fuckable, even though someone should give her some advice on how to dress.

At dinner, we happen to start talking about women. The Baron recounts to me all his woes, including his wrong marriage and lack of ability. I promise to do what I can with his wife to help him to get back his virility. (Naturally, it is my intention to fuck her.) At that, he gives me full liberty. I planned to leave the next day, but he makes me promise to stay for two weeks at least. He will see that I have company with other guests.

'Come now, my dear Baron, your company is sufficient for me. Whom do you think you are going to bring here? A couple of bores and prudes. You are the only charming person I have come across in these parts.'

'I think you can bring me back into contact with youth,' he admits.

The next day, I accompany the Baroness on her stroll. Her husband cannot be with us for he is suffering from a cold, but he almost forced me to get ready the Horns to be placed on his head. I don't lose any time. After a few vague preliminaries, I come to the point.

'I hope I shall not offend you, Madame, when I state that I did not come here without an ulterior motive. That motive was to be pleasing to you. I love you and I want you to love me. If you have any inclination for me, let us make arrangements. Get revenge on that tyrant of yours. I offer you consolation, assistance, delights, and a warm heart. Lovely Baroness, your reply will decide my lot. Your piteous condition should remove any indecision on your part. If I am unlucky enough not to find favour in your eyes, I'll leave.'

'What the devil! One is not that abrupt with a lady of breeding.'

'You're quite right.'

'You're incorrigible.'

We seal the bargain with several kisses, and she goes off to make arrangements so that she can spend the night with me.

How stupid it is to sleep with a woman when the man is on top. It is so monotonous. But she insists. I am petrified.

'The cure says that it is the only right way.'

But in two hours, she is climbing all over me. We finally separate, promising to meet again during the night.

The Baron does not suspect a thing, and she gives

me more money than I could expect from a provincial woman.

But, where did she get it?

Quite simple. Husbands in the country generally put their wives on an allowance. But my oldster is madly in love with his young wife and he gives her the key to his coffers. Without his knowledge, she removes two hundred louis which she presents to me. They are for my travel expenses. I then take my leave with the Baron horned and content. There are tears in the eyes of the Baroness as I get in my carriage.

My final rural excursion is at Salency where a bucolic festival is being held. The touching simplicity of the spectacle went to my heart. A young girl comes to bring me a rose. She is fresh and delicious and about sixteen. She gives herself to me freely. Never have I enjoyed such innocence. Not for anything in the world would I have paid for her favours. It has been so long since I have made love without financial transactions involved.

So, you are on the banks of the Lignon?

I gather that you are afraid of sheepfolds. What is wrong about relaxing in the arms of artlessness now and then? She was so enticing. And fresh. I still remember the naive way she mounted me. The heat from her mouth transmitted into mine is still there. Her eloquence was that of nature. We don't speak much. If only you could have inserted your hand into her bodice. Never would you have come across such delightful globes. They are firm and elastic at the same time. If only I could reveal to you her alabaster body. She had the contours of the Venus of Medici. Her skin was peaches and cream. Naturally, I have an erection. Her first scream is, 'How that hurts!' Her second is: 'How good it feels!' The way her adorable bottom wiggles and bounces is a delight to see. She does not yield but meets my attack courageously. Now she is returning thrust for thrust. When she discharges, every fibre of her body is affected. Her caresses become more animated. Her tongue darts lubriciously into my mouth. There is not a part of our bodies which does not serve as a venereal sanctuary. She is intent on her own pleasure, but she does not forget mine.

'You are the first one to make me feel what love really is,' she tells me one day. 'None of the boys here in the village is your equal.'

I blush modestly.

All things must come to an end and I leave this peaceful, innocent place. At the gates of Paris, I feel all of my old wickedness returning.

But one gets rusty in the country. There one talks all the time about morals, virtue, honesty and honour. Those people would have ruined me. I mentally count those whom I am going to turn into suckers. What money I am going to squeeze out of them! How the fuck is going to flow! But who are going to be my victims? I think I'll despoil our sisters at the Opera. I know I shall have both money and pleasure. After all, it will be merely retaliation. Let's pillage those who rob us and fuck those who fuck us.

Inspired by this noble sentiment, I hasten to the Opera. There have been many changes in the last three months and I have to get my bearings. I find myself in the dressing-room where all the nymphs nearly suffocate me with their kisses and embraces. I am grabbing breasts and bottoms.

'Where have you been? The story went that you were dead, devoured by wolves, castrated or converted, which is the same thing.'

I finally manage to disengage myself to go up to a charming ballerina.

'Hello, Mimi.'

'No. I am angry with you.'

'Come now. Let's make up. I would like to give you my virginity.'

'I don't want it. I'm in love with my patron.'

'What do you take me for? I am no novice.'

'I'm going to remain faithful to him.

'Who's talking about infidelity? How about going to bed with me tomorrow?'

'Suppose he finds out?' she laughs.

'How silly can you get?'

'He's old and jealous.'

'All the more reason to cheat on him.'

'He is a very important nobleman.'

'Damn it, he'll be nothing but a poor fool. If you don't agree, I'll give my all to Rosette. What would you say to that?'

At that threat, she readily accedes to my demand. I then go to dine with a banker who has some twenty male guests of distinguished name and boring conversation. This company is augmented by fifteen young girls.

'Horrors! You are back in your evil ways. You promised to renounce these creatures.'

'I'm keeping my word. My intentions are purely

dishonest. All I'm going to do is extract some money and bleed them a little.'

'But your trade is dishonourable.'

'There is no such thing as a dishonourable calling when it provides a living. After all, those fellows owe their fortunes to some whore's cunt. And those strumpets, don't they owe us everything? Who forms them in the art of perfidy and treachery unless it is us courtiers? We debauch a girl and take her away from her parents. Then we enroll her in the music academy, after which she can lift her head high while leading a life of vice and sin. But her heart is still innocent. What a delight to corrupt it! It is one of our favourite diversions. When we have finished, we congratulate ourselves on the result. In fact, we are praised to the skies.

'But that's not all. I would like to corrode the last remaining germs of virtue and poison the blood stream. I want her to be a pitiless corsair with a greedy soul. She will never know what gratitude is. Moreover, beneath her enticing exterior will be concealed the blackest of hearts. I want to inject into her all of my wickedness and teach her to take full advantage of a victim when he is defenceless. Then she will be able to fly on her own wings, snatching young men from the arms of their sorrowing fathers and weeping mothers. She will be sufficiently astute to bring wealthy merchants to penury and persuade husbands to abandon loving wives. We shall laugh together at the havoc we have caused as we share the spoils.'

Picture to yourself a brilliantly illuminated chamber with the doors locked and the drapes drawn. The women get down to the buff. What a charming sight meets my eyes. One, plump and dimpled, offers me a dazzling bosom. Another, a stunning blonde, resembles the Venus of Titian. A third is an alluring delicate nymph. What do we do when the signal is given? Why, we all start masturbating, of course. It won't be the last time for me, I assure you. All of a sudden, the atmosphere becomes charged. Voluptuousness is reproduced in myriad forms. There is heard the murmur of sighs, the sound of groans, and the swish-swash of copulation. The couches are creaking, tears are falling, and spasms seize the bodies. All are drowning in deluges of sensuousness.

What a tableau! How to describe fifteen women discharging simultaneously?

Now the orgy begins with free-flowing champagne exhilarating the participants. The tribades become true bacchantes. There are two in the sixty-nine position busily arousing one another. Take a look at that group twisted in the most bizarre formation. One lass is stretched out on a sofa with six admirers. She has her tongue in the cunt of the first who, suspended above her head, drenches her face with fuck and then stimulates herself by rubbing her cunt on her opulent bustiness. Then she is had from behind by the clitoris of a particularly lusty miss. Another, her head ensconced between the rounded thighs, is eagerly tonguing her grotto. Finally, she is revived by a dildo in both apertures.

They look as if they have gone berserk. And they are all ladies of breeding.

I go to spend the night with Mimi whom I find in bed. She has been expecting me. I quickly undress and am beside her. At first, she is somewhat shy, but my caresses dissipate her bashfulness. I enjoy myself thoroughly. You know the deliciousness of fresh fruit. I barely have enough time to employ all the twenty positions I know best when I hear a scratching on the door.

'Your cat is locked up.'

'Oh, let it stay there,' she breathes.

'All right.'

After a gratifying night, I get up at eight in the morning, leaving my lovely to continue her slumber. When I unlock the door to the bathroom, I find there the Chevalier de *** with only his shirt on. He is half-frozen and looks forlorn.

'My friend, how happy I am to see you,' he squeaks as he embraces me. 'I think I am dead.'

'What happened to you?' I inquire.

'I was in bed with Mimi when we heard a noise. She said it was her patron and squealed that she would be lost if I were found with her. I hid under the bed, and then I made my way here. I started to ponder how I could make my escape since I had no clothing. He is an old man, but he does have servants. I heard him fuck her. At least twelve times. My God! He must have stuffed himself with some aphrodisiac.'

'That's impossible,' I interject. 'Even I can't do that.'

'I repeat. Twelve times. I counted them. Finally, he left, but I was locked in.'

'I think you're making this all up,' I laugh.

He protests that it is the gospel truth.

'I think he fucked her in the rear,' he adds.

'That's enough, Chevalier,' I tell him sternly. 'I'm not a buggerer.'

'Well, who's talking about you?'

'You.'

'I?'

'Yes, you, for it was I that you heard.'

I leave him with his mouth gaping.

Our liaison runs its course, but I need more than a good romp in bed. Mimi is well endowed with diamonds, furnishings and cash. She gets an income of a thousand ecus a month, not counting the gifts. That is about fifty thousand francs a year. And I don't get a sou out of it. What good are those diamonds? They are not in fashion. Should I borrow them and sell them? No, that is not feasible. There is a Count who had his suspicions about me. Perhaps I could pocket the jewels and deny that I took them. It is damnably difficult to be a rogue today, because so many people of quality have adopted this code. I suppose the best way is to be an honest man. I'll have her hold open house with magnificent dinners. She will pay. When the jewellery and money are gone . . .

When the plan is put into effect, the polite world gathers in the house that is now *ours*. All Paris buzzes about our dinners. We have the prettiest girls and couples with the most outlandish apparel. There is a Knight of Malta who has brought back from his caravans only the most depraved Asiatic tastes. Although he is well past sixty, his only pleasure is with the young. The nascent fleece on a *mons Veneris* shocks him. What does he think he can do? Even whips on his withered buttocks fail to restore him to life. All he does is slobber piteously at the entrance of the sanctuary which he cannot penetrate.

Take a look at the abbot next to him. Are you blushing for him? He has a prick like a mule's and is as unscrupulous as he looks. No matter, he will get his mitre. Regard the carbuncles on his forehead and the veins on his nose. He grabs Martin, who well realizes that mice have only one hole and lets himself be taken.

Turcaret is getting sentimental. But just wait until the candles are extinguished. There he is now on top of Quincy, in whose hand he has placed his engine.

'Why are you always so timid?' he whispers angrily.

'I suppose that Mademoiselle Rosette will lend me her intestines for a fee of a hundred guineas,' Milord *** remarks.

'Go ahead and take her. I hope you won't be disappointed.'

D'Orbigny is giving satifaction to Colomba with his hand. She looks so respectful.

'Listen, Hortense,' says the Count, who is going to Rome. He is somewhat tipsy for the trip. 'You've given me gonorrhoea, but I suppose that's the way it is. I'm not complaining about that, but you've infected my lackeys and valets. That's disastrous for me.'

She looks remorseful and gives him an excuse. Soon they are together again.

Mimi gives balls with the added attraction of gambling. Young people and old children lose their all. Mimi is not happy. Within two months, we have consumed the trinkets, cutlery, diamonds, money, and furnishings.

While this is going on, a master butcher offers to keep her. Since I do not want to stand in the way of my beloved's future, I discreetly withdraw to attach myself to Violette.

You know that pretty little thing with a body that must have been shaped by the Graces. Her amazing bust consists of two perfect hemispheres. In addition to these allures, she has the unequalled talent of deceiving her patron. One has to be careful with her.

Her present protector is a gouty banker quite unable to meet the needs of a healthy young woman. Moreover, he is ugly as the devil and all he talks about is money. But every time he comes to see her, he brings a present. In a short time, we are rolling in money. In order to avoid unpleasantness, I have Violette pass me off as her brother.

One day while the Croesus is dining with her, I enter with a downcast expression. He asks my name and my employment.

'Monsieur, I am a tapestry worker,' I tell him.

'Do you know how to read and write?'

'Oh, indeed, I do. I spent three years in school.'

'I have kindly sentiments for your sister, and if you behave yourself, I'll have some for you, too.'

He slips two louis in my hand.

'He's a handsome boy,' he says to Violette. 'He has your eyes.' He turns to me. 'Do you have a mistress?'

Bashfully, I lower my head and twist my hat in my hands.

Violette cannot stand her lover. He bores her to tears. I do my best to make up for it during the night, for Monsieur's chaste spouse does not let him out after dark. Two ways of fucking particularly delight

213

my sweethcart, and since I invented them, I'll describe them.

After the first two times, because you have to be warmed up, you seize your lovely and place her slightly diagonally on top of you. Then you pass your left arm in the gap caused by her position. With your hand you massage the left breast. She will be fucked dog-fashion, that is clear, but her head, bent down on yours, will enable you to put your tongue in her mouth. Your right hand rests on her clitoris. Imagine all that going on at once – the mutual movement of the two hinges, the busy tongues, and the gnawing teeth. Even the most frigid women are driven out of their minds. I must say that Violette does honour to my discovery.

But my name will not pass on to posterity. Ungrateful mortals, you honour with laurels and panegyrics those who bore you. To the shame of France, there are no prizes for those who are master fuckers. Monks and priests without testicles are esteemed and given rich livings while I enjoy my prick with no praise except from my partner. In days of yore, Apollo played the lyre with his prick.

What I propose is an academy of fucking, which will be the glory of France. Each member, to be elected, must have invented a new position or variation. There will be awarded a prize to the most graceful method of fucking and a gold medal to the best one performing it. The judges will be a duchess, a stewardess, a ballerina from the Opera, and three whores. Then we shall see the flowering of priapism, a superior religious faith. Fucking instead of prayers will be the form of worship to that highest of deities.

Violette has the most beautiful hair in the world, and she has a mania for being fucked in her tresses.

Being fucked in her hair?

What's so surprising about that? You can fuck in armpits, eyes, and in ears. It is impossible with her bosom, for her breasts are too firm and far apart.

But here is what I do. The little Messalina stretches out with her legs spread. Putting my feet where I should have my head, I fuck her in the mouth. Then with my head between her thighs, I do *minette* to her. You would die laughing if you could see us.

Monsieur Duret continues to provide us with money, which I take care to see that all is spent. Our debauchery clubs give me a certain amount of amusement. It goes without saying that he does not take part in our meetings.

One fine morning, I go and ask a little hussy I know if I can lunch with her. The servants are never around and I get into her bedroom without any difficulty. A significant noise makes me realize that she is occupied. I am retiring when I hear her cries.

'That's enough, Reverend. Enough! You bugger of a monk, you'll kill me.'

'On my honour, I just want to finish my daily dozen.'

He is one of us. Picking up a julep, I wait until he has finished his litany. Then I open the curtain.

'Father,' I say very humbly. 'Wouldn't you like this cooling drink? You seem to be very hot. Heavens, what a prick! I have never seen anything to equal it.'

It's none other than Father Ambroise, in charge of a mission.

'Let's be friends,' I continue. 'Here, we'll have a drink together and you have nothing to worry about.'

Reassured, he continues his rutting.

'This is the result of our robes,' he tells me. 'I hate them. Beneath them we conceal pricks of iron and hearts of chicken, for fear of the frightful punishments that await us.'

'Punishment for having fucked a pretty woman?' I innocently inquire.

'No. Only if we are stupid enough to be caught. But we bring many benefits to many homes where the husbands are indifferent or incapable. As long as the peccadillo remains secret, we have nothing to fear, but if it comes out, we are sequestered.'

'You mean you are locked up?'

'Yes, I had to pass the sentence once myself when I caught a young padre with Madame Dumas. Since we live on charity, hypocrisy is our second nature. We practise a thousand frauds to support our indolence and vices. To tell you the truth, we are not worth a damn.'

'For your age, Father, you have come far,' I remark.

'That's true, but let me tell you why. I entered a seminary at the age of nineteen. There I thought the devil was lurking in every corner. The thought of his horns frightened me out of my wits. Since I have been here, I have put them on many heads. In the name of sacred obedience, I was buggered. Since I was big and well built, I became the favourite catamite of the order. At the same time, my prick attained the eminence which you now see. Because I was desirable both in front and back, I was presented to the archbishop who was visiting our cloister. After measuring me, he honoured me with the supreme mark of his favour by turning his rump to me. I entered the abyss which stank to the high heavens. As a reward, he gave me permission to become acquainted with cunts.

'Then he took me to Spain, a marvellous country where there are many blossoms to pluck. I prefer milk-white flesh, but a monk cannot be too choosy. I won't tell you how many beautiful girls we imprisoned as Jews and fucked as Christians. We gave them absolution with our pricks. Unfortunately, we had to burn at the stake about a dozen because we were not sure if they would tattle or not. Yes, discretion is the noblest of the virtues. Father Nicholas died a martyr's death – syphilis. I performed several services for Cardinal Carrero, who made me a vicar. But I soon tired of the life of a bugger. I was high enough in rank to indulge in my own tastes without any fear. I fucked, I fuck, and I shall fuck. That's the end of my story.'

We sprinkle holy water on him.

'Father, do your devouts pay you?' I wanted to know.

'Of course. I generally make about a hundred pistoles a month. I guide cunts as well as consciences.'

'What about confession?'

'A perfect occasion to instruct a pretty girl and tranquillize an overly respectable matron. You certainly are stupid for a man of the world. What sense is there studying Saint Augustine or Duns Scotus? Drinking and fucking are much more enjoyable. We titillate the old women and give pleasure to the young.'

'But, Father,' I object, 'what about the sanctity of the family?'

'That is where we shine most brightly. For a woman, no matter her age, to have only one man is sheer stupidity, and we point that out. We literally ruin families by knowing all their secrets. If there is a young girl I want to fuck and she is reluctant, I see to it that she is swallowed up in a convent where she can repent her excess of virtue. If a woman's fiancé does not surrender to me, I break up the intended marriage by spreading rumours that he is impious. I see to it that he is disinherited, and all that for the greater glory of God. I give comfort to the wife who wails the night through because of the impotence of her disgusting spouse, and when I am through with her, I see to it that she is disgraced and dishonoured. Let's have another drink. As they say, *in vino veritas*. But I warn you that you had better not betray the secrets of the church. You'll be sorry.'

'I, Father? But I am not dependent on you like the others.'

'You're not dependent? We'll see about that. I won't stand for being insulted.'

'Stop it, you villainous monk,' cries Alexandrine. 'You fuck like an angel, but you have the soul of a devil. I am disgusted and I don't want to talk to you any more.'

'You're biting the hand that feeds you, but go away. I am not hard now.'

He turns to me. 'Do you think we would attack you openly? Of course not. We would begin by going to your friends and praising you highly. But we would mention certain faults. The seeds of suspicion would be planted.'

'But I would not give you any hold on me.'

'It makes no difference. People love to gossip and believe the worst. There would be anonymous letters which would be avidly read. Your enemies, and everyone has some, will be delighted.'

'But I could defend myself,' I assert.

'I am sure of that. But as Machiavelli remarked, always slander, for at least a scar will always remain. It is infallible.'

'Indeed, Father, I never realized how crafty and clever you are.'

'We have to be to exist,' he modestly replies.

'I have almost a mind to take orders.'

'You could do worse. From talking with you, I think you have a definite talent for our calling.'

After this edifying conversation, I leave him with Alexandrine in bed again, and return to Violette. She tells me that Monsieur Duret has lost all his money. We don't have a sou. I tell her to sell her furniture to pay the debts, and I leave her in order not to disturb her while she is breaking up our household.

Since I love music, I take refuge with Gaymard. The bitch is ugly, but she has a good voice. Also, she fucks like a madwoman. Because of my reputation, we are able to cut short the preliminaries. I agree to six times a day. She dismisses her water-carrier, whom she has worn out, and allows her lackeys and hairdresser to have some peace. We decide on a common purse (with the understanding that I do not have to contribute anything to it). She gives recitals and receives guests who eat her out of house and home while despising her.

My life is spent with musicians of varying talents, but my ogress is starting to tire me. She swears like a trooper and has no manners. All she can do well is fuck. One final trick decides me to give her up. One evening after the theatre, I go to her house. She is going to dine in town as I am. But can one leave without having one's boots greased? I sit on a chair and when she gets on me, I fuck her. At the peak of pleasure, she pretends to lose her senses, which, in reality, she does not. I have a fine watch she has always wanted. She gets the idea of purloining it. She deftly lifts it and puts it in her pocket. I notice what she is doing. In turn, I manage to obtain possession of hers, which is extremely valuable. We are even.

The next day, she is very worried but I am completely at ease. I tease her a little.

'You are shameless,' I tell her. 'Here is your watch back. You can keep mine because you have profaned it. My sole vengeance will be to tell everyone about your kleptomania.'

While she is making all sorts of excuses, I bow and depart.

I decide to make Dorville my sultaness. Indeed, she is worthy of the honour. A nymph figure which is gently rounded, peaches-and-cream complexion, and big blue eyes which beg me to kill and then revive her. We sleep together in her house, and the first night is decisive and eloquent. I establish myself as master of the household.

This new arrangement pleases me very much. Every day there are new refinements in the art of love. One morning, I find her as she comes out of her bath. She is like Venus emerging from the waves. Adorned in nothing but her own beauty, her tresses flow down her back while her hand caresses a bosom of alabaster.

With a pleased smile, she contemplates her charms while reclining in a chair. As I witness this voluptuous spectacle, I become aware of a stiffening in my trousers. Flames race through my veins.

The rustle I make offers me another tableau. With a deep blush, she bends down and attempts to conceal her nudity with the locks of her hair. At that moment, her toy poodle leaps down and takes position before her grotto, yelping ferociously all the while. Laughing until my sides burst, I enter and console my beauty, and one does not have to be told how.

I suppose you think I have every reason to be happy. Well, I am not. Within this temple of beauty, Dorville encloses a capricious fury which is constant only in evil and foulness. She attracts lovers merely to devour them.

'I am irritated,' she tells me one day about some innocent she has plucked clean, 'that I left him eyes to weep with.'

She corrupts everything. Her perfidious tongue distorts the simplest things. Under a veil of ingenuous naïveté, she hides the most treacherous of souls. She is capable of any crime as long as she is sure she is not going to get caught.

Well, why do you live with such a monster?

I don't know. Perhaps because she is seductive. I thought she loved me. Well, I pay heavily for the mistake.

One of my friends, Count *** has been coming regularly to see Dorville and his presence does not constrain me. I did not think he had his eye on her. Gradually his usual good humour disappears to be replaced by gloom and moodiness. I feel sorry for him, and when I try to cheer him up, he repulses my advances with a coldness that presages a rupture. I take Dorville into my confidence and ask her help. She agrees. The traitress!

A few days later, she alarms me with her mournful appearance. Then I surprise her as she is shedding hot tears. I keep after her until she tells me what is bothering her.

'My dear, my heart is breaking. If I tell you why, you must give me your word that you will keep your temper.'

I promise.

'You thought that the Count was your friend,' she says. 'Well, he's nothing but a Judas.'

'You can't mean that,' I exclaim.

'Yes, he is a coward and traitor. He got on his knees and told me he loved me. I tried to dissuade him. I told him to think of his friendship with you. I reminded him of honour. He swore that his former friend was now his enemy. I can't repeat the terrible things he said about you. My heart was bleeding.'

Again she is racked by sobs. Her tears bathe my visage. Now her fumblings stoke the fires of voluptuousness and jealousy. I feel a new sense of indignation. My pride is aroused and I vow to avenge my honour. Under the guise of trying to appease me, she puts more fuel on the fire. I am seething within.

When the Count appears, I provoke him. Dorville prevents any explanation of my ill humour. The situation becomes so unbearable that the Count insults me. After I slap him, there is only one thing to do, and we do it. I get him with my first lunge and he is stretched out at my feet, his sword on the ground at his side. Forgetting our animosity, I kneel at his side and try to stanch the flow of blood gushing from his breast.

'There's nothing you can do,' he whispers. 'I am dying and I deserve it, for I tried to kill you. Dorville asked me to.'

'Dorville?' I am stunned.

'I wanted her so badly that I would have done anything for her. And this was her price. Please forgive me, and let me die still your friend.'

With a final attempt to embrace me, he expires.

Seized by a senseless fury, I make my way to Dorville's house with the sword still stained by my friend's blood.

'Well, I killed him,' I shriek. 'You wanted me to murder him and him to slay me. Well, you got part of your wish.'

I see an expression of serenity and even joy on her face. She even dares to stretch out her arms to me and congratulate me on my victory.

'You termagant, you had better tremble for your life. This hand which you have rendered criminal may punish you.'

At this threat, uttered in a menacing tone, she gets on her knees before me. Her cheeks take on an ashen colour and her bosom heaves convulsively. When I throw my rapier aside, her self-confidence returns.

'Yes, I arranged it,' she admits. 'I loathed him, but I led him on so I could get rid of him. So I turned him against you. I knew that you would be in no danger, for he is not much of a swordsman. He offended me a number of times before, and now I am revenged.'

I scarcely hear what she is saying. Wearily, I leave her and go home, where I immediately gain my bed.

For a long time, I am inconsolable. I avoid all human contact. Never can I get out of my mind the memory of my friend's last moments. I am so depressed that I long for the rest of the tomb.

In my house in another apartment lives a colonel's wife. She leads a retired existence. Because of my dissipated life, I have never come to know her well, only exchanging an occasional greeting with her. Becoming worried about my state of mind, my valet has the idea that the young woman can distract me. He tells her chambermaid about me and this is repeated to the Marquise. Her curiosity is piqued. When she learns the cause of my lassitude, she is genuinely touched. Every day she asks about me. When she comes to inquire about my health, I am so apathetic that I am unable to thank her.

One day, as I am going out of my house, we meet. I hasten to make amends for my lack of courtesy. We soon became bosom friends. For all practical purposes, I live in her apartment. Her understanding and comfort gradually assuage my grief. But I have to watch out for love. A companionship between a charming young woman of twenty-two and a man not advanced in years is bound to lead someplace. Moreover, sorrow is always susceptible to tenderness. The inevitable occurs.

She is attractive without wishing to appear so. She has a kind heart and a good head. But she is not happily married. Like many military men, her husband neglects the treasure he possesses to chase the frights that hang around encampments. Nevertheless, he is a brute who demands absolute fidelity from his wife.

What a difference there is between the caresses of a woman like the Marquise and the tarts one meets in polite circles. The latter may provide temporary diversion, but when it is over, there is a bad taste in the mouth.

The Marquise is in the flower of young womanhood. If she did not have such a perfectly proportioned figure, she would appear to be a giantess, for she is almost six feet tall. I have never seen such a ravishing bosom. There is a delightful irregularity about her features which I find irresistible.

She turns off the compliments that I contantly rain on her.

'My friend,' she tells me, 'if you keep on like this, I'll be as vain as a peacock.'

Perhaps because she is both chaste and pure, I have never known such heights of pleasure.

The battles I must fight to conquer her virtue! I keep telling her that love is no sin. Dare I admit it? For a long time, her sense of respectability is stronger than my desire. She senses the danger. She even writes her husband to come and be with her so that she will not yield to temptation, but he dismisses her pleas. For her pains, all she gets is indifference and insults.

I launch one last attack and I am successful. She no longer blushes when she is with me, and peace reigns in the house. Who can blame her for her defeat. For six months we live in paradise. We are sufficient unto ourselves. When the fires go out, they are immediately ignited again. Constantly we discover new charms in each other.

How long can bliss last? We are nothing but the playthings of destiny. It is not long before my Marquise is bearing the fruit of our love. Soon her condition can no longer be concealed. On his return to Paris, the husband soon finds out about our affair, which he immediately divulges to his cronies. The insults he hurls at us! I am ready to exact vengeance, but Euphrosia restrains my arm. Now the happiness is gone. She weeps all the time.

'Euphrosia,' I tell her one day, 'how I regret that I cannot lessen your grief. I suppose you hate me.'

'Hate you?' she protests. 'Nobody has ever been so dear to me. This poor child I am carrying will be born under unfortunate auspices, but at least it has tied more tightly the bonds that unite us. I have no regrets for what we have done. I am afraid that I have little to offer you now. I do hope that this infant will remind you of its mother.'

'What are you saying?' I cry in anguish. 'Is that how you show your love? Go ahead and die, my cowardly mistress, but before breathing your last, you'll have the cruel satisfaction of seeing the demise of your lover. So you're going to deprive your child of our tender cares and leave it a target of the darts of fate?'

Euphrosia interrupts me with her sobs. Her flood of tears seems to give her some relief from her grief.

'Darling, let's banish these funereal thoughts. Courage. Keep going for the sake of love. Haven't you told me a thousand times that you lived just for me?'

She promises to pull herself together.

A few days later, I have to go to Brittany on a short trip. But Euphrosia's pregnancy is becoming more pronounced. I have gloomy forebodings. Our farewells are shot with misgivings. We feel that it is the last time that we shall see each other. She faints when I get into my carriage.

I conclude my affairs quickly when I receive a letter from a friend: 'Return instantly. Don't lose a second.'

Dropping everything, I hasten back. A black wreath is hanging on Euphrosia's door. My God! She is no longer. I want to see her and kiss her one last time and then die with her. Ignoring the attempts of those who try to hold me back, I advance. They speak to me, but I do not hear them.

'Stop, young man,' a venerable gentleman orders me. He is coming out of my beloved's rooms. 'Have respect for this site of sorrow.'

I am moved by his severe but gentle tone, and I kneel before him.

'Whoever you are, please have pity on me. Permit me to see one last time my mistress. That is all I ask of you. Afterwards, I demand nothing but to die to be with her.'

'Get up!' he commands me courteously. 'You are hurrying me to the grave, you young idiot. What have I ever done to you? Until now, nothing has besmirched my white hair, and now you want to expose me to shame and disgrace. Your dastardly affair has cost me both my son and daughter. The one was my support and the other my happiness.'

'Are you her father? Heavens, take your revenge for

227

my having taken your daughter. I won't deny the love
I had for her.'

'Although I have lost everything, I cannot blame
you for my woes. I can't find it within me to hate
you.' My sobs are my only reply. 'Now don't take it
too hard. Euphrosia is still breathing.'

'I have to see her. Oh no, you are just saying that
to get vengeance.'

With those words, I sink back senseless, not hearing
a word, in an armchair. Euphrosia's father takes me
by the hand.

'I am speaking the truth, but that does not mitigate
the cruelty of our lots. I wish you to listen to the
misfortunes which brought all of this about. A week
after your departure, my son-in-law came to see his
wife who was telling her brother about her love affair.
When he heard about it, the Marquis became furious.
My son tried to calm him down, but it was in vain.
The Marquis threatened Euphrosia, even by trying to
beat her. My son threw himself in front of his sister
to protect her. When the Marquis refused to desist,
my son drew his sword and wounded him. Then the
Marquis pulled out a hidden pistol and fired. The
bullet killed my grandchild. At the sight of the
horrible happenings, Euphrosia fell into a dead faint,
giving a stillbirth. For a time, the mother's life hung
in the balance, but today she seems much better. But
how will she escape her grief?'

Without making a movement, I drink in this
horrible recital.

'So, she's alive, but I know that she detests me. On
the other hand, she can't hate me. Let me be your
son to make up for your sad loss. Gladly will I assume

228

the duties. I promise that Euphrosia will live to love you.'

The old man is obviously moved. He sees a ray of hope.

'We are deluding ourselves,' he says. 'Euphrosia is coming back to life, but her life has been poisoned for ever. She refuses to talk to me and hides under the covers. She threatens to go to a convent.'

I do my best to dissuade her, but she is adamant. A few weeks later she pronounces the vows and takes the veil.

I am so depressed that I decide to go to a Trappist monastery, resolved to spend the rest of my days there.

But the gods are against me. A thunderstorm forces me to stop at Verneuil. I am soaking wet without a change of clothing. When I am in bed, I am in the depths of depression and contemplate suicide. Suddenly, cemeteries seem lovely places to me. I see the rows of crosses. The chimes from the church tower seem to presage my death. I desired death, but fate was not of the same mind.

Absorbed in my own reflections, I do not notice the pretty young maid. I snap myself out my revery, only to fall into another. The girl asks me what I would like to have for dinner. When I look at her blankly, she thinks, rightly, that I am slightly mad. Finally, I focus my attention and exchange repartee with her. We both laugh.

I order. Madeleine goes up to remake my bed. When she returns, she allows me to see a well-turned leg. The gods are smiling on me. But, I repeat to myself, I am destined for the grave. Well, why should not this delightful little creature benefit from me before I am buried? She'll be the last fuck of my life.

I throw her on the bed have her skirt up to her neck before she can utter a word of protest. She makes a sign of resistance, but what woman can complain after she has received the third thrust? She wiggles as if she has the Saint-Vitus dance. As usual, I would like to begin again, but she tells me that she still has to work. But we agree to meet again together that night. I give her a few louis for I shall have no further use of money.

We spend the night together. It is the last time for me. She is a little vexed at first, but after her fifth homage, there is not a whimper out of her. She is thrashing about as if she were out of her mind. As usual, I am ready to start all over, but she protests, saying that she is expected below. But she quickly returns.

A miracle occurs. The more I go in and out of that carmine-rimmed hole, the more calm I become. My resolve weakens, and I decide to put off my plan until the next night.

The next day at dinner, two men join me. Great is my astonishment when I see that they are my closest friends.

'What's wrong with you? You look like the last rose of summer,' exclaims Saint-Flour.

With that, they tease me mercilessly until I have to laugh along with them. Finally, I am persuaded to go back with them to Paris.

For a time, I am at a loss as to what to do. To add to my difficulties, I am deeply in debt, and my creditors with their hangdog looks are camped on my doorstep. Finally, I make a momentous decision – I am going to get married.

It is the end.

I am acquainted with an old woman who knows everybody. I go to her and tell her what I want.

'Do you want her pretty?' she inquires.

'That's unimportant,' I say airily.

'Do you want her to be rich?'

'As wealthy as possible.'

'Intelligent?'

'It would help.'

'I think I have the right party for you,' she declares. 'Do you know Madame de l'Hermitage?'

'No.'

'I'll introduce you. She's one of my best friends, and she has an eighteen-year old daughter. She has lots of money and a lovable character.'

My amiable duenna leaves immediately to make the overtures. Two days later, I go with her to meet my future mother-in-law. She has the figure of a skeleton and the bearing of an empress. She overwhelms me with compliments. As the two hags exchange idle talk, I examine the salon. Rich tapestries cover the wall. An enormous chandelier is suspended from the ceiling. In every corner and nook are antiques. All in all, it speaks of a wealth that tickles my cupidity.

My go-between and I leave. She tells me that I have made a favourable impression and that in all probability I will be invited to dinner to meet Mademoiselle Euterpe. What a name!

I receive the expected invitation and meet my promised. She must have been carved with a hatchet with a monkey as a model. She is the spitting image

231

of her mother. When she smiles, she is even uglier. My God! Am I expected to marry that?

So you're not going to take her as your wife?

Well, she has forty thousand livres for an income, and all I possess is a fine prick which she'll hardly ever feel. My creditors are yapping at my heels, and I suppose I have to immolate myself.

After fifteen days, we exchange the marriage vows. An annuity of twenty thousand is settled on me. After the ceremony, my wife goes to the nuptial couch, where I find her huddled under the sheets. She is weeping her heart out.

'Madame,' I tell her, 'marriage is a hard road which can lead to happiness. The roses lining the way are not without thorns and it is up to me to pull them out as your husband. Our Lord has joined us to make us one. In order to complete His task, He has seen fit to equip the man with a peg.' (I put her hand on it, but she withdraws it in terror.) 'Now this has to find its hole, which is in you. Allow me, please, to look for it and then plug it.'

I take hold of my Christian who squeezes her thighs tightly together. When I start opening them with my knee, she punches me in the face with her fists. Finally, she raises her derriere and I am knocking at the door.

Now the gate is flung wide open. I rush in. She is scratching me like an enraged cat and yowling like a maniac. The sputtering mother comes bustling in, but she soon calms down.

'My son-in-law, I know how it is,' she says.

'I know better than you,' I retort.

'Don't worry. It was the same with me on my wedding night.'

'To hell with your whole family.'

'Don't say that. She's just a child. She'll come around. Win her over with gentleness.'

'Let the fucker who began her take her back. She's as big as a mare.'

'I suppose it is because you are incapable,' she remarks with a frown.

'What do you mean, I can't? No trouble at all. You could drive in there with a carriage.'

The old hag gets angry again. I ignore her and storm out of the room, leaving that cursed house forever.

The story gets around. The sarcasm will be the death of me. Where can I flee? Where can I hide?

That's not all. The following day, a man dressed in black asks to have a word with me. He shows me a document.

'Monsieur, you are mistaken,' I stammer.

'No.'

'From whom is that?' I ask.

'From Mademoiselle Euterpe de l'Hermitage, your lawful wife.'

'If you don't get out of here . . .'

He beats a hasty retreat when he sees my threatening fists.

The bitch makes a legal demand for me to treat her as a wife. If I don't, she insists on an annulment. I rush to my lawyer and we fight for three months in the courts. In the end, I am deprived of ten thousand livres income and declared the father of a child with whom the monster is pregnant.

In desperation, I abandon this miserable country where I have met with so many misfortunes. Never again shall I insert my prick into a marital cunt. To get vengeance on the world, I am going to fuck all of nature. There won't be a virgin left on the face of the earth. Legions of cuckolds will people palaces, cities and fields. I'll exercise my rights even on the Virgin Mary. And when I descend to the paternal arms of Monsieur Satan, I'll fuck the dead.